MELINA GRACE

Unveiled

The Healing Clone, Book 3

BY MELINA GRACE

The Caris Chronicles

The Last Seer (A prequel)

Things Unseen

Underneath

Surrendered

The Healing Clone

Unviable

Unknown

Unveiled

For Trixie, Caleb, and Mal.

Gotta mix it up as Trixie is sick of always being

last just because she's the youngest

MELINA GRACE

Unveiled

The Healing Clone, Book 3

Chapter 1

"It is with great sorrow that we gather to remember the life of a brilliant woman. It is the greatest tragedy, and we grieve tremendously the death of Cynthia. She was taken from us too soon."

I stare at the ground, trying to ignore the gloating in James' voice as he speaks over the fresh grave a few meters in front of me. I don't look up. I don't want to see Liam who is once again standing at James' side. *His right-hand man* as James likes to call him. Bile burns my throat.

I feel for Adam and the others who were close to Cynthia. Their grief is deep, and they don't deserve to have this occasion marred by James. But what can we do to stop him? In the six months since we got here, he has gradually gained more and more power over the group of clones hiding in the large cave that once felt like such a safe haven.

Tears prick my eyes. I don't pretend to myself that they're because I'll miss Cynthia. I hardly knew her. But they are for my loss. Loss of hope that I'll be able to convince the Resistance to come to the aid of The City; and sympathy for my friends who I've grown to love, for their loss of Cynthia.

And the loss that hurts the most, though I know it shouldn't be as important as the other two—the loss of Liam.

I hardly see him anymore. He's always by James' side, and I avoid that power-hungry man as much as possible. Perhaps more than the loss of Liam's companionship, I grieve the loss of my respect for him. How can he support someone whose values are so wrong in every way?

Adam steps forward, and I realize James has finally stopped talking. I think Adam will say something now, maybe share a memory about Cynthia. But he doesn't. He merely drops some wild flowers on her grave and turns to leave.

"Don't go far Adam. You'll need to fill this hole in as soon as possible. It will be easily visible from the air," says James.

I see Adam's shoulders stiffen, but before I can step forward to stop him, he's turned and is swinging a powerful punch toward James' face. Guns are raised, and Liam steps forward intercepting the punch and knocking Adam down.

I wince at the thud as Adam's head hits the rocky ground. I step forward to stop Adam from picking a fight with Liam he could never win, but Adam doesn't rise. He's out cold. James smirks. I turn accusing eyes on Liam. He stares impassively back. I try to find the man I once thought I knew in his cold stare, but he isn't there. I wonder if he ever was.

Carla and Brody help me lift Adam to carry him back to the cave. Someone else will have to fill in Cynthia's grave. I wonder whether the others will get a chance to leave their flowers and say goodbye, or whether James will insist the grave be filled immediately.

Paige rushes after us, and we make room for her to check Adam's vitals as we continue to carry him. It's a fair walk to the cave. Jack and Carla found a shaded spot around the back of our mountain that had a pleasant view and earth that wasn't completely rock so we could dig a deep enough grave for Cynthia. It's well out of sight of the road so people can visit her grave if they want to.

Paige steps away from Adam, giving us room to maneuver him through some boulders. She seems content that he's okay. I don't know how she can tell. He doesn't seem that different to how Cynthia was when we first got here—unconscious with a large lump on her head.

I hope he wakes. Cynthia never did, and though the nurses were able to get soup into her, she slowly deteriorated over the months until she finally died two days ago.

We're halfway to the cave when James and his cronies catch up to us and shoulder past. I see Liam, who's just behind James, snake a hand out and grab Adam's wrist.

"Haven't you done enough already?" I ask, unable to keep the venom from my voice.

He pulls his hand back and, without sparing me a glance, continues on his way.

I grind my teeth. "Let's stop for a break," says Carla. I happily comply. The more distance between me and James and Liam, the better.

We move Adam into an upright position and hold him up between us.

"Did it work?" Adam slurs.

"Nothing works anymore," Paige replies, moving over to him. I look at her in surprise. Paige is usually so quiet and compliant; I would never expect to hear a word of dissent from her.

"Let me see your eyes sweetie," she says, lifting his head from its lolling position.

"My head hurts. He wasn't supposed to hit me in the head," Adam mumbles.

"He wasn't supposed to hit you at all," I growl.

A strange look passes between Carla and Brody.

"He's quite confused. That's to be expected. His eyes aren't good either. We'll have to keep him under close observation for signs of a concussion," says Paige.

"I'll stay with him tonight," Carla says quickly.

"That won't be necessary. I can," Paige replies.

"I'll stay with him too," Carla says firmly.

"James won't be happy if you miss your rotation," I say. Not that I really care what James thinks.

"James can stick it," says Carla.

"James is the one who said our well being is of the most importance. He'll have to act as if he cares about Adam's well being," says Brody.

I look at him in surprise. Not because I disagree with him, but I'm surprised to hear Brody say it. Brody is usually the confrontational one; in fact, I'm even more surprised it wasn't him that took the swing at James rather than Adam who is ordinarily more diplomatic. It's unlike Brody to think about what James needs to do to maintain his appearance of concern. Brody never cares about appearances, only about what he thinks is right and what he believes should be done.

He's had more than one altercation with James and his cronies over the last few months. Though come to think of it, it has been a while since the last one. I search his face as we help Adam stand. I wonder what's been going through his mind lately. There are a few people who've been acting out of character; my thoughts drift to Liam again.

The walk back is long, and Adam moans through much of it. He continues to make confused comments. It's Carla and Brody who are acting the strangest though. A couple of times Carla begins to say something but is cut off by Brody who gives Paige significant looks. I don't know what's going on between the three of them, but I don't give it too much thought. My mind is racing, and my emotions are in turmoil. The Resistance is falling apart around me, and as much as I love the people here, I can't find any justification for staying much longer. I can't help them against James. They'll need to work out how to help themselves. I need to help my family in The City, who have a much larger danger looming over them.

A light weight lands on my back at the same time as something rolls into my legs. I stifle a laugh, though it's unlikely anyone will hear me this far from the farm we just left. I can't see who the culprits are that almost bring me to my knees in the dark, but I recognize Sonja's giggle as she clings to my back.

"Scoundrels! I almost dropped the fruit. You're both going to get it!" I threaten them.

"I'm soo scared," Sonja replies as she leaps from my back and races into the dark to retrieve her heavy sack.

"You should be!"

My words are light, but my heart is aching. I don't want to leave these people. I've been raiding the countryside with the little people for the last six months. At first they needed my direction. Even though I knew virtually nothing about gathering food from the farms and orchards, what little I knew was volumes more than the little people, and they needed me along as a scout. We'd had help from a few others who knew a little more than me, but it didn't take long for the little people to catch up with all they knew and then they'd gone on to do other jobs during the day. I managed to stay with the little people by avoiding James and claiming that if they're discovered, we'll all be at risk. He's barely tolerated my reasoning. Everyone knows how good the little people are at hiding. I really should have more faith in them myself; I just worry about them.

I've spent the last few months teaching them how to fight, but as their little stunt, just then, shows, they are just too small to be effective. Though, admittedly, they were playing nice with me. If they meant business, they would have been leaping on me and punching me in the throat and gauging my eyes, not just trying to tackle me down.

I sigh again as children giggle around me. I'm really going to miss this mob. I wish I was leaving them with someone better than James in leadership, but at least they have somewhere safe to stay and know how to find food for themselves. I hope one day to see them again. I would love to bring my family out here, though the dream of returning has soured somewhat now that I won't be able to share that future with Liam. I shake my head. Who he is and how I could have been so deceived about him is a mystery I don't know how to unravel.

We get back to the cave well before dawn. I haul the fruit back to the 'kitchen' and sneak back out to the large front cave while the little people are organizing our cache. They're used to me not helping as I can barely see anything in the dim light they prefer.

I grab the pack I prepared yesterday and sling it over my shoulder. Pausing at the entrance, I peer around the dark cavern. Most people are asleep, and I can only really recognize them because I know where they usually bunk down. I'm surprised to not see Carla sitting up in the shadows, but Adam was doing well before I set out with the little people, so I suppose she didn't feel it necessary.

A part of me longs to say farewell to Liam. Once upon a time, I believed he would be making this trip with me even if no one else was. He's in one of the back caves though, with James and the rest of his cronies. My nose curls; even if he was here, I don't have anything to say to him anymore.

Turning my back on my friends, and the cave that once held such high hopes, I crouch down and creep out into the brisk early morning air.

Chapter 2

A loud roar echoes along the ravine. I look back over my shoulder but fail to see what's making the noise. At least I'm downwind so, hopefully, whatever's out there doesn't catch my scent.

I quicken my jog, using the moonlight to navigate the rocky ground. There doesn't seem to be any caves nearby, though getting cornered in one of those would probably not be a good idea anyway.

Another roar echoes from the other side of the ravine—closer this time. Did the creature really gain that much on me or is there more than one of them? Either option isn't a good one.

A roar replies. They're getting closer, and, yes, there is definitely more than one. I look back over my shoulder, and this time I see it. It's an enormous cat-like creature with a mass of hair obscuring its face. I can't make out much of its features, but the large eyes, glistening in the moonlight, are clearly visible staring at me.

It roars again, and I don't need any more urging to break into a sprint.

More roars reply. There's a pack of them!

I haven't run far before my breathing is coming thick and loud. I haven't exerted myself that much, and I suspect my shortness of breath is mostly due to fear. Those animals look powerful, and they sound terrifying.

Another roar tells me they're getting closer. They're definitely following me. I frantically search the ravine walls for anything that might help me escape. Even a small cave or hole I could block up with large rocks would offer some protection until they lose interest.

It's hard to see anything in this light when I'm running so fast. There's a dark patch on the wall up ahead. I veer to the right to try and make out what it is more clearly. The animals are big. If I can find a cave small enough, they won't be able to follow me in.

I crane my neck, trying to get a better view. My foot catches on a rock, and I pitch forward. Gravel scrapes the skin from my arms, and I'm thankful for the trousers that protect my legs. More roars behind me hurry me back to my feet. I momentarily worry about them catching the scent of my blood, but it's too late for that. They already have me in their sights.

The dark patch on the wall disappears as I approach it and I realize it's just a shallow indent. I continue sprinting down the ravine, my head turning in every direction as I try to find anything to help me and trying to keep a better watch on the uneven ground.

A roar just behind me almost makes me jump out of my skin. Maybe that's their skinning tactic. Scare their dinner skinless.

A nervous giggle escapes me. Well, I'm calling it that, though I have a sneaking suspicion others might call it hysteria.

I throw another glance over my shoulder. Three of the large beasts are just behind me. Even with my quick look, I'm able to see the muscles bulging in their agile legs. I have only seconds before one of them pounces on me.

Not for the first time, Dominko kicked himself for not taking a sample from Sample before he let the soldier steal her away. He didn't even smile at the irony of taking a sample from a Sample. No wonder Finn had reacted so much to her name. Dominko was beginning to question a lot of the things he was raised to believe normal.

He pushed his microscope away in disgust. He was just frustrated because his research wasn't progressing, he told himself. He wasn't getting sick of genetic engineering. Why he needed to keep repeating that to himself, he wasn't sure. He needed genetic engineering. If he didn't have his research, then what would he have?

His father had finally lifted his grounding, but it hadn't made much difference to Dominko. He'd considered finding a beautiful woman or two and taking them out for the best night they'd ever had, but the thought just made his mouth go dry. What was the point?

He tapped the desk, looking around for inspiration. He'd reached a wall in his research and exhausted every avenue he could think of. He'd head home and reread Falisco's notes. Maybe he'd missed something the first sixteen times he'd read them. His mouth quirked to the side. As if that were possible. He'd always had an eye for detail and extraordinary comprehension skills. Still, he could hope that there was something in Falisco's involved notes that had an implication he hadn't yet registered. He shook his head at the unlikelihood of it. He had nothing better to do though, so he raced for the stairs. For some reason, he'd become quite adverse to the confined space of elevators. He chose to ignore the obvious metaphor of how confined his life felt. It was nothing but ridiculous that someone with access to so much money, travel possibilities, and license to pretty much do whatever he wanted—could feel trapped. *Ridiculous,* he reiterated.

He had more freedom than most people in the world, a lot more than the average citizen, and certainly a lot more than the clones did, he thought with a painful clench in his gut.

Well, it's not like there was anything he could do to help them. He didn't have any real power. His dad had all of that; and besides, everyone liked the way things were. As long as the unviables were in The City, people could forget they were there—out of sight, out of mind. As long as there were clones being made, there would be unviables, even he wasn't clever enough to get a clone perfect every time, especially not in the early stages. And they had to put the unviables somewhere. They couldn't just be left to wander around without a purpose where they might hurt someone.

Dominko's forehead creased. A small doubt shoved its way through his reasoning. Was it right? His head hurt at the question. It wasn't the type of thing he was accustomed to considering.

Is it fun or challenging? Now they were questions he knew how to address. Unfortunately, nothing seemed fun anymore. His genetic engineering was the only thing challenging enough to keep his interest, and besides if he could create more healing clones the world would be a much better place. He longed to see people healed of the things that ailed them. It was one of the things he loved about Sample—her power to relieve people's suffering.

He started to jog. His shoes slapped against the hard ground, and the sun beat down on his exposed neck. He wasn't dressed for running, but he needed to escape his thoughts. Maybe he should start driving to work again. The twenty-minute walk afforded him too much time to think.

As he ran, his mind emptied. He focused on the steady slapping of his shoes on the ground. The shoes weren't ideal, but it felt good to run outside for a change instead of in the gym. He ran straight past his apartment complex. The sun, warming his skin, lifted his spirits and he didn't even care that his good shirt would get sweat stains.

He started to become aware of his surroundings. Not the buildings or the gleaming path. They held nothing of significance; they were the same stagnant, practical things they had always been. But there were other things of interest around, one might even say beauty. Flowers lined the feet of the buildings, all different colors for spring. There was a cat atop a wall and a bird flying through the air. As he watched them, genetic symbols began to play through his mind as if he were watching a movie. With every creature he saw, a new equation fell into place. Things he'd never considered before. At first, he thought it was just the overload of information he'd crammed into his head. He'd thought of nothing else and done nothing but look at engineering codes for weeks, but the connections just kept coming. Yes, it was the equations he'd been studying, but now he was making assessments that had never occurred to him before.

And then it dropped. The information he'd been searching for. It had been there all along; he just hadn't realized the significance of it or how to apply it.

His eyes cleared and he realized he was standing still on a busy corner with people passing him on all sides. Some of them were looking at him strangely; well, he guessed, not so strangely. Their looks were probably pretty fitting given Dominko's behavior. He grinned at a man in a wheelchair. "I'll be able to heal you," he said.

The man scowled and rolled past. Nothing could dampen Dominko's excitement though. He'd finally figured out how to make more healing clones. He laughed out loud. "I just needed some fresh air!"

Chapter 4

I drop to the ground and let my momentum carry me into a roll to the side. I come up in a crouch facing the large beasts who are bounding toward me. I'm astonished at how quickly they change direction. They're only meters from me.

Surely I can't miss from here. I level my gun at the closest one and fire. I try to block out the sound of its roar as I level my gun at the second. I don't have time to pause or think about my aim. I only hope I've left myself enough time to shoot all three.

I fire at the second as the first crashes past me. And then I'm shooting at the third. I get the shot off before the second huge cat crashes into me. Sharp claws rake across my arm ripping the gun from my grasp.

From the corner of my eye, I see the third cat bunch its legs beneath it and, with a deafening roar, leap toward me.

I kick the second, weakened, beast and manage to fight free, jumping out of the way just before the third cat lands heavily where I was. I crouch into a fighting stance, but it doesn't rise. I take a deep breath; my bullet must have found its mark before the beast leaped.

I look around for my gun but can't see it in the moonlight amongst all the rocks. Pain lashes through my arm, and I think I catch a glint of white bone.

The first cat rises and turns its head toward me. Solemn eyes stare at me. I start backing away up the side of the ravine.

The beast is between me and the way I was going. Glancing around, I search for the best way to get past it. Reflected light draws my eye, and I see my gun—too close to the beast that has me in its sights. I really want to put another bullet in it but I'm under no illusion that I could possibly retrieve my gun without being ripped to shreds by those horrifying claws, and my other guns are buried in my pack. I run higher up the incline and, checking that the terrifying creature isn't following me, begin to circle it.

Having put some large rocks between the ferocious animal and me, I check it one last time. It's nudging one of the other cats with its nose. Hopefully, it's too injured to give chase, but I break into a run anyway ignoring the pain lancing through my arm. I want to put as much distance as possible between me and those beasts.

I don't get far though. My ravine comes to a sudden end. A gaping hole splits the earth in two. Way beneath me I see a rushing river cutting its way through the mountains. Once again, I wonder if I did the right thing coming this wild way instead of following the roads. It seemed like a good idea at the time, but I can hear more roars behind me, and with no way forward, I think taking my chance with enforcers or Clone Industries would have been a better bet.

How many of those beasts are back there?

I race across the ravine to the other side and begin climbing the incline. Hopefully I'll find a place to stop and make a stand on the other side of the ridge.

I can't even feel the rough rocks cutting into my hands as I climb. Even though I try to only use my good arm, the pain in my shredded arm is unbearable. The smell of blood makes me feel like prey, and I'm beginning to suffer dizziness.

A loud roar draws my attention upward. One of the cats stands at the top of the ridge above me, proudly silhouetted against the sky.

Stopping where I am, I look back the way I came. Sure enough, one of the beasts is down there too, and I can see more advancing toward me along the incline. They move with a stealthy grace that belies their huge size, treading the steep and rocky slope as easily as if they were walking down a smoothe road.

I'm about to sit and empty the contents of my pack where I am. As unfavorable as this position is, it seems this is where I will have to make my fight. I know I can't possibly beat them. Once the fight begins, they'll be upon me before I can shoot them all down. With the cliff directly behind me, they won't even have to still be alive for their momentum to carry me over the edge. I take one last hurried look around. My eyes are drawn by the sheer drop to the river below.

The beasts are good on a steep descent, but they don't have hands. Surely, they won't be able to climb down that?

I shake my head at the foolishness of what I'm about to do. If I was in good health and there was no raging river at the bottom, then this might be a good option. But, with one arm an agonizing mess, I don't know how I'll hold myself to the wall.

Dropping to my belly, I lower myself over the edge.

As if realizing I'm escaping, the cats let out a concerted roar and bound toward me.

I hurry to lower myself out of their reach. A scream rips from my throat when, in my rush, I reach out with my mangled hand to support my weight. I'm not holding on with anything else, and my ruined fingers give out.

I fall.

My body scrapes along the cliff face sending agonizing stabs of pain through my shredded arm. I tear the skin on my good fingers as I grab at rocks trying to find purchase.

I grab a small outcropping and arrest my descent. My ruined arm hangs limply as my feet shuffle around the cliff looking for anything they can stand on.

I should have taken my boots off before attempting this. 'Cause I had time for that. While I was at it, I should have brought some grappling hooks, picks, a sling for my arm, and ropes. My feet finally find purchase and I press my body into the wall. Resting my face against the cool rock, I breathe out a shaky sigh.

A roar from above draws my attention. There are three cats at the top of the cliff, not that far above me. They are prowling around like they're trying to find a way down. What is wrong with those things? Surely there's easier prey around?

I risk a look at my arm, trying to assess the damage, but I can't see much in this light or from this angle. I raise it up to get a better view of it, ignoring its throbbing protests.

Four deep gouges run the length of my forearm and hand. Blood wells from them and drips freely into the nothingness below. I gape at the sight. I need to wrap it before I lose much more blood. If it wasn't for the adrenaline hyping me up, I'm pretty sure I'd be unconscious by now.

I search the cliff face and find a small ledge not too far away. Biting my lip, I angle toward it. I can't climb without two arms, so I use my shredded one as little as possible, and always make sure I'm putting most of my weight on at least one of my feet.

When I finally get there, I find it's a lot smaller than I thought. I wrestle my pack off my back and onto half the ledge. Managing to turn around, I perch half my bum on the ledge beside my pack while my legs dangle over the edge. I concentrate on keeping my center of gravity well back while contemplating my pack. It's on the wrong side of me.

A moan escapes me. Everything just feels so hard at the moment. Geez, I wonder why that is? I giggle and lean my head back against the rock wall. I just want to stop. I'm so tired; it's becoming difficult to think straight.

My eyes open with a start. I need to get my arm bandaged. I've lost too much blood. If I lose consciousness here, I'll fall to my death even if I don't bleed out.

Carefully, I reach across my body with my good arm and grab my pack. It doesn't usually feel this heavy. With a lot of careful shuffling, I manage to swap sides with it. I resist the urge to have a short break and reach inside for some material. At this stage, I don't care what I use. I just need to get something wrapped around my arm.

I pull out a black top. The effort is almost enough to undo me. Leaning back against the cliff, I close my eyes for a moment. That only makes me more aware of the pain lancing through my arm. Gritting my teeth, I start wrapping the shirt around my arm. I bind it tightly, trying to pull the skin closed in an attempt to slow the bleeding. I pin my arm to my body in an effort to stop the material from unwinding and rummage through my pack again. I pull out my only other top and knot it around my arm, holding the material in place.

Job done, I lean back with a sigh. The tight bandaging is causing my arm to throb even worse, but I'm relieved to have stemmed most the blood flow. My eyes droop closed again, and I force them open. I take a deep breath of the cool night air and survey my surroundings. I have to stay awake while my body heals itself. My ledge is too small for me to balance on if I don't maintain full concentration.

The sound of rocks falling draws my gaze upward. You've got to be kidding me! One of the cats has started making its way down the cliff! It perches on a tiny ledge staring back at me.

"What is your problem?" I ask.

It doesn't answer, but after staring at me a moment longer, it looks around and leaps to another small ledge.

"This is beyond a joke," I mumble, as I look around me seeking a route away from the persistent beast. I don't suppose it matters which way I go, no direction leads anywhere safe. Well, I guess back up to the other cats is the worst option and I don't really feel comfortable veering directly under the large cat. It's so crazy, it will probably just leap down onto me and take us both to our deaths.

I remove my boots, shove them into my bag, and choose the only direction that offers some handholds. I have to use my wounded arm to get from one precarious rock or divot to the next, but I make very sure to never put all my weight on it. I can ignore a lot of pain, but I can't force torn muscles and tendons to do what they can't do.

I ignore the cats following me down the cliff face; ignore the fact that I don't have a safe destination in mind or any plan of how to escape the beasts. I focus just on the wall, on keeping my breathing even, of choosing the best grips and footholds, on the next place I need to place my wounded hand or searching foot. Everything else fades into the background. It's just me and the climb and the cool night air caressing me.

I angle diagonally down the cliff until the sound of rushing water is a deafening roar beneath me and then I keep climbing down. I don't know what I'll do when I reach the bottom, but there are no other options available to me, so I keep going.

I stretch my foot out, seeking another hold, but I can't find one. I move it in every direction searching for something;

only smooth rock meets my chilled, bruised, and torn skin. I pull my foot back and rest it on its former perch, taking a moment to appreciate the relative comfort of having all four limbs bearing my weight.

Leaning back as far as I dare with my uncertain handholds, I search for another grip. Nothing but smooth wall reflecting the moonlight glistens below me. There's no purchase within reach to the side of me either. The cats have fallen behind, but I'm dismayed to see they're still arrayed across the cliff face above me.

I find a likely route heading back up but away from where the beasts are making their way down. It amazes me how they can jump so far from one ledge to the next without falling. It mustn't be easy for them because it takes a long time in-between jumps for them to make the next leap;

 and yet they keep coming.

There's nothing to be gained by staying where I am, and so I begin climbing back up, thankful that I'm still able to angle away from the cats.

It's close to dawn when I near the top. I pause, debating what I should do. If the cats are all on the cliff face, then I can climb up and run away and gain some distance from them, but if there are still some up top, then it won't take them long to chase me down. I look around for a different direction and am dismayed to see plenty of small outcropping rocks leading away along the rock wall. I don't want to climb anymore. My arm is throbbing, and all my other limbs are shaking from fatigue.

I'm going to have to take my chance above, or I'm likely to fall to my death. The top looks much farther away now that I've decided to climb there. Clenching my teeth, I concentrate on moving my injured hand to a small rock above me and then move one of my feet to follow.

It slips.

Chapter 5

For a moment, there's nothing but air around me. I grab a tiny shelf with my good hand and manage to wedge a foot into a crevice. Taking a deep breath, I rest my head against the cold cliff face. I'm glad I'm going up and not continuing this treacherous climb.

When I reach the top, I almost start crying. It isn't a top at all—just a small rocky ledge running along the cliff with another incline rising above it. I look up. The rise above me isn't as steep, but it looks to be covered in loose rocks—my least favorite surface to climb.

Turning around, I search the ledge and rise for any sign of the beasts. I can't see any. Though, I have noticed they camouflage well with the sandy rock, often not being visible until they move.

Climbing up onto the ledge, I pull my flask from my belt and take a quick swig of water before starting to hurry along the ridge away from the horrifying cats. Loose rock litters the ledge, threatening to roll under my feet and pitch me over the cliff. Nevertheless, I make much faster headway than I was making before. It's a relief to put distance between me and the beasts, but I know the safety I'm feeling is an illusion. They will catch up with me easily once they reach the ledge, and I'll be forced back down the cliff.

I pull a protein bar from the side of my pack and begin to gnaw on it, but I know it will not be enough to give me the energy I need to escape my pursuers or to enable me to take on that cliff again.

Perhaps the river will be more crossable here. I lean out over the edge to get a view of the water below. But I'm running too fast, and I misjudge, leaning too far.

I begin to fall.

Flailing my arms wildly, I throw myself back against the rocky incline behind me.

Loose rocks slide from beneath me, but I lean back and manage to keep my position. My breaths are coming in heavy gulps now. Looking around, I see a huge tan cat pull itself up onto my ledge.

I pull a gun from my pack and loose a couple of rounds. It's still too far away for the bullets to reach.

The river below is still a raging torrent, and I know I won't be able to last on the cliff face indefinitely, especially as the beasts won't just give up and leave but will follow me down. The cats will catch me too soon if I stay on the ledge, so there's only one direction left. I begin to climb up, digging my toes into crevices and trying to find rocks that won't give as soon as I put any weight on them.

The incline isn't as steep, forcing me to weight-bear on my legs and just use my arms for balance. It's much easier on my arm, but I'm in constant fear of the ground sliding away from beneath me.

The mountain seems to reach forever above me, and I can hear the cat gaining on me. I ignore the fact that I have no destination in mind. No safe haven waiting for me; just an endless climb and the certainty that the beasts will have to catch me in the end. Despite my throbbing arm, aching body, and bone-numbing fatigue, I continue to climb. I will not give up.

When the cat is close enough, but not too close this time, I turn and shoot it. Three bullets hit it in the chest. It doesn't even roar, just quietly collapses and slides down the incline and over the edge. I listen for the sound of it hitting water, but don't hear anything. I can't even hear the sound of the river from here. It's such a high cliff, the thought of the cat falling that great distance chills me even more than climbing the cliff face had.

I look around. There are no other beasts in sight. A small hope surfaces that I've left them behind.

With a little more energy, I begin to climb again, angling away from where the cats were following me.

I climb until the sun has risen and its harsh light glares off the rocks, blinding me to the way ahead. And then I climb some more. It's harder than ever to see whether the sandy colored cats are still following me, though I check regularly.

I make it to a small ridgeline, take a short break, and then begin climbing again.

I'm halfway up the third incline and considering following the next ridgeline away, instead of continuing my climb, when I hear another roar.

Somehow, one of the cats has managed to get above me.

"Crap." Where do I go now? I glance back down. There are more coming into sight along the ledge below.

I pull my gun out and begin to fire. One of my bullets clips the animal above me. It lets out a deafening roar. Instead of stopping, however, it bunches its muscles beneath it and leaps down the incline toward me. When it lands, it knocks a large rock loose that rolls down the rise knocking more boulders loose and gathering in speed.

The rocks above me aren't moving yet, but falling rocks keep knocking more and more loose in an ever-increasing area. I start to run along the incline. I could fall at any step, but I'd rather slide for fifty meters than get caught under those rolling rocks.

I'm not fast enough.

I've only gone a few meters when rocks start sliding down on top of me bruising my shins and threatening to knock my feet from under me.

Turning to face them, I see larger ones descending on me. They're hard to make out in the cloud of dust that surrounds them.

A large boulder descends on me at rapid speed. I jump to the left, narrowly missing being squashed. I land on my elbows and scream at the impact on my injured arm. Skin is torn from my other arm, but I don't have time to worry about the pain. More rocks are descending on me.

I leap to my feet as a thigh-high rock reaches me, surrounded by rocks on either side of it. I jump over it and crack my knees on another descending rock behind it. Large rocks are rolling down the hill all around me, and there's no safe direction to take.

Dust fills the air making it hard to breathe and see. Coughing, gasping for breath, and squinting against the dust in my eyes, I leap up again. I land on a boulder and without stopping to think, leap for another large rock heading my way. The rock slides from under my feet, but I'm already moving, flying toward another boulder crashing down the hill.

I continue to leap from one boulder to the next, barely daring to breathe the dust filled air that billows around me. I can't see more than a few meters, but that doesn't matter as I wouldn't be able to pick a route anyway. All I can do is pick out large rocks to leap to. I choose them a few in advance, planning my next leap before I land.

I keep jumping for what seems like an eternity but is probably only a few minutes.

Finally, I bound onto solid ground. Well, there are still loose rocks everywhere, but at least they're not flying down at me.
The slight give under my feet feels heavenly compared to the precarious footing of a moment before. I scramble upward, putting as much distance as possible between me and the still falling rocks below, and seeking clearer air. My chest is aching, and I realize I'm holding my breath. I let my cough out and with lips barely open, risk a gentle intake of air. Dust particles stick in my throat, but I manage to resist coughing further. I keep moving upward and begin to breathe in fresher air.

Collapsing onto a relatively rock-free patch of dirt and wedging my feet against a couple of firmer rocks, I lean back against the incline sucking in gulps of fresh air. I pull my flask from my belt and manage to get one last drop from it. It's not enough to soothe my raspy throat. I have another flask in my pack, but do I dare use it? With the unreachable river below the only water around, I don't know how long it will be before I can find more.

I can feel another coughing fit coming on, so I relent and dig my other flask out. I take two long shallow gulps; enough to rinse my dirt coated throat, but no more. I bury the flask in the bottom of my pack so I won't be tempted.

My eyes are full of dirt, and my hands are also caked in fine sandy stuff, as is every piece of clothing I have and both the outside and inside of my pack. I clean a hand as best I can by rubbing it against different things and then try to wipe some of the dust from my eyes. I only succeed in getting them to water. I lean back again and with my eyes closed, wait for the tears to do their job. My dehydrated body can't produce enough though, and the few drops just succeed in aggravating a few grains that rub between my eyelid and eyeballs. I try to rub them out again and manage to make one eye feel better though now the other feels scratched.

I give it up for a lost cause and begin searching my surrounds.

I gasp as big solemn eyes meet mine. Only meters below me, one of the enormous cats perches on a precarious ledge. He watches me with an uncanny intelligence. He's leaning against a large boulder and when I look closer, I realize his back leg is trapped beneath it. My rapidly beating heart begins to calm again.

I look around in every direction, but I can't see any of the other beasts. My gaze returns to the trapped cat. Now that it no longer threatens me, I can see it's a creature of amazing beauty. I take in its sleek lines that, while at rest, hide, what I know to be, impressive muscles. Its face is kindly and its eyes full of intelligence. It's hard to believe that only moments before it was trying to kill me. That it was, in fact, relentlessly hunting me for half the night and into the day.

I need to get moving before any of its friends catch up. These cats seem to have an uncanny knack for surviving in these mountains. I look around, searching for a route, but my eyes keep returning to the cat who still watches me with its large solemn eyes.

I can't help it. Even if I knew how to get it out from under that boulder without squashing the both of us, it would undoubtedly turn straight around and try to eat me.

Lifting my pack, I push myself to my feet and choose the path of least resistance; the path that will lead me away from the massive beasts and these mountains, and back to the flatter land near the main road. My eyes are drawn to the cat again. I pull my gun out and walk toward the creature. I should at least put it out of its misery. I can't just leave it to die a slow death.

It lowers its head and rests its chin on its paw, not in the least concerned that I'm advancing toward it. Maybe it doesn't realize that I'm holding an instrument of death in my hand. I don't get that feeling though. Rather, it almost seems to be welcoming what I'm about to do.

I get to within a couple of meters from it and stop. I don't dare get any closer. I've seen what those paws, now so cuddly looking, are capable of. It gazes at me and, for a moment, I lose myself in its deep eyes.

I find myself circling the boulder until I'm behind the cat and have a clear view of the back leg and where it's trapped. There's a drop just beneath it. It really wouldn't be too hard to edge the boulder in that direction. It could all go wrong, though, and crush the animal. But, really, it's not like it's going to be any worse off.

I circle back to the front. This is stupid.

I give the cat my most threatening stare. "If you try anything, I'll shoot you dead."

I advance slowly. The cat doesn't move. Its head is still resting on its paw. Only its eyes follow me. I reach the boulder.

I'm within swiping reach now.

I put my good shoulder to the boulder and push. At first, it doesn't move, and I'm about to give it up for a lost cause. I can't take the time to try to find a lever. But then I hear a crunching sound and the boulder begins to move, slowly at first; but then it drops away.

With its resistance gone, I fall. Within moments the cat is on top of me; its massive weight pinning me to the ground and its hot breath panting into my face.

I've dropped the gun and can't even manage to wiggle my hand to find it.

Chapter 6

Dominko hummed as he danced naked around his apartment. He'd had a new large mirror installed in his lounge room that gave him a good view of his chiseled torso whenever he passed it. The window screens were open allowing the morning sun to enter and anyone at a high enough vantage a, what he believed to be, glorious view of himself. Indeed, he passed close to the windows frequently allowing those lower down the opportunity to admire him as well.

Poached eggs with hollandaise sauce for breakfast tasted better than ever, and he was eager to step out in his new suit. He loved it when his tailor was in town.

Everything seemed delightful on this beautiful spring morning. He fancied he could even hear birds chirping. He was finally making progress on the healing clones. He had his first samples started and had great hopes they would prove successful. He'd already started working on some improvements for the next batch. He would start looking for some nurturing clones to tend the samples for the first few years of their lives, and for a facility, isolated from people, for them to live in. He wanted it to be more like a home than the usual dormitories. These clones would be special with an extraordinary function, and they deserved to be raised in a way that would encourage that.

A harsh beep came from his phone, signifying that his dad was calling from one of his scrambled numbers again. His dad had thought he'd beaten Dominko with the last program his techs had come up with to hide his caller ID, but Dominko had been able to write a counter program to recognize his dad's hidden signature.

Dominko laughed. Nothing could get him down today. "Hello daddy dearest," he sang into the device.

"Dominko!" His father's voice cracked like a whip over the phone.

Dominko frowned. Not even a sigh to signify his dismay that Dominko had foiled him once again.

"What have you been doing?" His father barked.

Dominko turned his head, searching his apartment for the cause of daddy dearest's anger. It was a bit concerning. His father never raised his voice. His anger usually took a quieter, though just as lethal, expression.

"Um, breakfast?" Dominko winced at his stutter. Never show fear, never show weakness. Everyone knew that about predators. Flippancy was his usual response to his father's ire, but the raised voice had caught him off guard.

"You've reopened the healing clone project!"

"Um, yeah." Dominko's caution gave way to excitement. "It's working father! I've managed to work out how to make them, and they don't send energy to clones—only humans, so they'll be able to survive under clone care!"

"So they'll only destroy humans you mean, not clones?" Carlos yelled.

Dominko failed to point out that technically clones were humans. He was trying to puzzle out what his father had meant by the statement.

"They're not soldiers, father; they're healing clones."

"The project is to be shut down immediately. I thought I'd eliminated any possibility of it being reopened last time. Whatever gave you the idea to start it up again?" Before Dominko could respond, his father had a fresh thought. "How were you able to get the information to create those samples again anyway?"

Dominko scrambled for a reply.

"You didn't go into The City, did you?"

Fear settled over Dominko. He wasn't sure what his father was saying, but he was sure it wouldn't be good for him, and it certainly wouldn't be good for Samuel if his father knew where he'd gotten Falisco's notes.

"Dominko! Where did you get the information? We don't even have the original computers that Falisco's files were on."

"No, but they were transported from a trash can with some other files. No one but me would ever have found them. They were erased from any casual observance, but I was just playing around one day searching out the mainframe's most erased files, and I happened across them." None of what Dominko said made the tiniest sense, but his father wouldn't know that; his affinity had always rested with engineering, not computers. He considered computers pleb work, and though he acknowledged Dominko's expertise, he had very little respect for it.

"Did it never occur to you that the project was closed down for a reason?"

"Um, no." Dominko could probably try to persuade his father that healing clones could only be a benefit to the human race, and indeed to his father, as he could make a lot of money from them; but he was no longer paying much attention to the conversation; he knew his father would never be convinced by anything he had to say anyway.

His device rested on the bed, his father's irate voice continuing to berate him. Dominko pulled his new shirt on. The style and craftsmanship completely lost on him as he rushed to get out the door. A sense of dread had settled deep in the pit of his stomach. Ringing Dominko wouldn't have been his father's first call of action. Dominko knew this was merely what his father considered a courtesy call, along with a command to make sure Dominko didn't repeat his mistake. No, if his father was calling him, it meant he'd already taken action to close the project down.

"Basement," Dominko ordered the elevator.

"What did you say?" His father barked.

"I was just talking to the elevator," Dominko replied.

"Report straight to head office," Carlos ordered. "Obviously, you've too much idle time on your hands. I'll be assigning your tasks henceforth." His father ended the call, sparing Dominko the hassle of making up an excuse for why he wouldn't be able to get there immediately.

Dominko jumped out of his Mustang and raced for the elevator. It opened smoothly, and a breath of cool air rushed out to greet Dominko. He had no time to appreciate it. "Labs," he ordered and then held his breath, waiting to see if the lift would comply. His wrist involuntarily pressed against his thigh, as if that could stop the elevator from reading his chip and his access permissions. Not that it would take him to the labs if it couldn't read his chip anyway. His breath released in a rush as the door wooshed open before him revealing the large front room of the labs.

He raced out of the lift and toward the side room where he had his samples. His heart thumped heavily in his chest. There were too many people here. People in generic gray coveralls. A man exiting his lab, his arms full.

"Hey! You can't be in there!" Dominko yelled. Heads turned toward him. Other geneticists, surprised at his uncharacteristic outburst. Dominko ignored them. He rushed toward a man who was stacking small boxes outside his door.

"Leave them be! They're mine!" He turned to the other man and grabbed at his arm, trying to stop him from leaving. "They're all mine."

The gray-clad man tried to keep walking. Another man with a clipboard exited Dominko's lab. "We're under strict orders to remove and destroy everything from this lab. The orders come from Mr. Dahlquist himself and can't be countermanded. You are not permitted to be here or to interfere," the man said to Dominko.

"No, No. There's been a mistake. You've got the wrong lab." Dominko felt a pang of guilt at his attempt to send the crew to one of the other geneticist's labs, but it didn't last long. None of their projects were as important as the healing clones.

"This is room C9?"

"Yes, but—"

"And you are Dominko Dahlquist?"

"Well, you know I am."

"And this is your lab?"

"No."

"No?" The man's head jerked up. He reached for his device. "I need to ring Mr. Dahlquist."

"You don't have direct access to him," Dominko hoped his statement was true.

"I assure you, this matter is of extreme importance to Mr. Dahlquist."

A light flashed on the phone, indicating it had heard the name and was ringing through.

"No, wait!" Dominko stalled. "I mean, it is my lab, but you've got the wrong one. I have another lab. That's the one you were supposed to empty."

"This is the lab we were instructed to empty," the man replied in a firm voice.

Dominko turned on his suave. It was time to take control of the situation. "Really, you don't think I know what lab you're supposed to clear out? It was me who requested *my father* get someone to do this menial work for me." He stressed his relationship to his father, hoping to remind the man of his influence. "Ha ha," his laugh sounded unconvincing even to his own ears, but he plowed forward. "You don't think my father would do this without my consent? Of course, we discussed it first. In fact, I just got off the phone to him before I got here. Why do you think I rushed down? I wanted to make sure you didn't bungle things, as you are so obviously doing."

"You are not supposed to be here, Mr. Dahlquist."

"Of course I'm supposed to be here. It's my lab. The whole place is mine. The whole building! You are employed in my company. You think my father makes these kinds of decisions without my input? I basically help him decide on everything that happens in Clone Industries." Okay he needed to stop. No one was going to believe that. Dominko was pretty sure he wasn't even aware of a lot of things his father was doing.

The gray-clad man didn't even have the decency to look skeptical; he just turned his back on Dominko and re-entered the lab room. "You are required to leave Mr. Dahlquist," the man said over his shoulder.

"No! Don't you know who I am? Don't you know who my father is? I'll be running this company one day and then what kind of job do you think you'll have?" Dominko could hear himself getting hysterical, but he couldn't stop.

"I'll pray for the health of your father," the man called out.

Dominko stood, mouth agape. *Was that a joke? Did he just make a joke?*

Dominko shook himself out of his stunned stupor. The first man was getting away with his computer. Dominko raced after him and began pulling the equipment from his arms.

"Desist," a deep voice ordered from behind him.

"I will not! It's mine!" Dominko replied with a quick glance over his shoulder. His head whipped back for another look, quickly followed by the rest of his body. Two hulking soldiers stood there.

"What are you doing here?" Dominko gasped. "Where were you hiding?"

"We were in your office sir," One of them replied.

"Why? Why are you here?"

"We are under orders to escort you to Headquarters sir."

"Whose orders? How did you know I would be here?"

"Mr. Dahlquist commanded us to wait here and, in the event that you showed up and proved uncooperative, we were to escort you to Headquarters."

"I'm not uncooperative. I'm completely cooperative." Dominko stepped back from the gray-clad man carrying his computer away. "See? I'm cooperating."

"Please come with us," the second soldier ordered, gesturing toward the elevator.

"No, no. You're only supposed to take me if I'm uncooperative. I'm being cooperative. If you take me now, you will be disobeying my father's orders."

"Mr. Dahlquist desires your presence at Headquarters sir."

Dominko stepped around them and bolted for his lab. Once through the door, he stopped dead in his tracks. The room had been demolished. They'd even removed his benches.

The fridges were gone. A quiet thump drew his attention to the side, where he saw a glass container full of smoke. He swallowed. They'd destroyed the samples. He looked around the room. Bits and pieces lay in an untidy mess, but there was nothing of any value left. All his work destroyed, and all the information being removed. He was under no illusion that he would be able to recover his computer. He might excel at kickboxing, but he was no match for the soldiers, who he could feel standing at his back.

There was nothing here. Nothing to stay for. Nothing to warrant continued disobedience of his father. He turned to the soldiers. "Let's go," he said. He headed toward the elevator, toward Headquarters, toward his father and his new tasks. A dead, black weight nestled in the pit of his stomach. He had thought he couldn't despise his father more than he already did, but this was a whole new feeling, one he didn't want to put a name to. He only knew his father would be ill-advised to meet with him alone in a dark alley any time soon.

Chapter 7

The cat's front paws are crushing me with its enormous weight, its eyes stare into mine. They don't look so docile now. Menacing, menacing is how they look—the eyes of a hunter.

My heart feels like it's going to explode from my ribcage. How could I have been so stupid? A low growl emanates from the depths of the beast's throat. I want to close my eyes. The enormous sharp teeth hovering only inches from my face are almost enough to make me wet myself. But I force myself to keep my eyes open. Whether daring the cat to take me on or begging it not to, I'm not sure.

Its front paws lift from me, and I wait for the swipe that will shred me. It doesn't come. The sound of stones rattling tell me the cat is moving farther away.

I leap to my feet, grabbing my gun on my way, and swing to face the cat. It's sitting a little away from me, watching.

Is this a truce? I could shoot it now. But then, why did I free it?

I start moving backward, waiting for it to decide it does want me for dinner after all. It makes no move to follow, and I start to move quicker. A stone shifting beneath my foot jars my ankle. Thankfully, it's only tender, not sprained.

I turn, and with frequent checks over my shoulder, hurry away from the beast. It lowers itself to the ground and, curling around, begins to lick its back leg.

The farther I get from the beast, the more I focus forward, and the less often I check to make sure it hasn't moved, though, my back prickles with the knowledge there's a predator behind me. The steep incline has less of the tiny stones, with hard earth, between the scattered rocks, now affording better footing. The loose rocks are the perfect size to turn an ankle though, and there are enough of them to require my full attention. Sparse and prickly bushes have begun to litter the slope giving the occasional firmer grip and making my trek less precarious. At least, if I start sliding down the slope, there's a chance of something to arrest my descent.

I get to a bend in the ridge and turn to look, for what I hope is the last time, at my cat.

Nine of the large beasts stand watching me.

My cat is half a head taller than the others, and I hope that means it's in charge. None of them seem like they're about to follow me. I lift my hand in a halfhearted wave and slip around the bend. What did I do that for? That was just weird. I hope my action doesn't incite the beasts to chase me.

My heart is beating rapidly in my chest, and I hurry forward. I don't trust the truce I seem to have established with the cats. What if they're just playing with me, giving me a head start, a sporting chance to reward me for rescuing their friend?

I've reached another ravine, which means much easier going than across the rocky incline. Unfortunately, the ravine is heading the wrong way. Heading back south, the way I've come. I need to go north or, at least, west to find a way across the river.

My arms and legs are shaking with fatigue. I pull some dried fruit from my pack, but even as I chew it, I know it won't be enough to give me the energy I need. I want to sleep or, at least, to sit down and rest. My back is still prickling, and I know I need to put as much distance as possible between those huge cats and me.

I look across the ravine to where the steep sandy incline above the river continues to the west. The cats are quicker than me on that sort of terrain, but they're quicker than me on the solid floor of the ravine as well.

I stare at the steep slope, the sun glaring from its treacherous rocks. My legs shake beneath me, and my arm burns with pain. I just can't face the slippery slope again right now, so I make my way to the floor of the ravine and begin to hurry along it.

The sun is beating down on me from above, and I'm glad I don't have to continue climbing across the steep slope where there was no reprieve from watching the ground and having the bright glare angle into my eyes.

I search the edges of the ravine as I hurry south. It's aggravating to be heading in the wrong direction but at least the going is easier, and I'm putting some distance between me and the cats. I look for a crevice or small cave or hidden overhang. Every shadow teases me with possibilities, but they all amount to nothing.

Until one does.

I draw level with the dark patch and still can't see where the wall flattens out. I move closer, my exhausted feet dragging in the dirt. It's a low, narrow cave. I want to crawl in, out of the hot sun, but Liam trained me too well in the mountains for me to risk that. The fleeting thought of him—and us, back in those days hurts. How could he be such two completely different people?

It's not worth mulling about anymore. I've left him behind and may never see him again, so it really doesn't matter anyway.

I dig through my pack until I find the small torch buried at the bottom. Pulling it out, I turn it on and flash it into the cave. I heave a sigh of relief; it's empty.

I contemplate some of the larger rocks in the vicinity. I had planned to block myself in so the cats couldn't find me. But I've seen the power in their limbs and anything I'm strong enough to pull into position, they'll be able to move away anyway.

"This is foolish." I'm under no illusion, they won't be able to find me if they want to, but I could run all day and through the next night and they would still catch me eventually. Only I can't. My wounded arm, the cliff climb, the twenty hours without sleep, the intense midday sun and the hours of fleeing have all conspired together to rob me of all my energy. I fall to my knees and climb into the hole.

I awaken with a start, banging my head against the low cave roof. I half lay down in the small space, rubbing my forehead. What woke me?

I don't have to wait long to find out. A loud roar echoes around the ravine through the cool night air. A gunshot follows. I jerk upright, again smashing my head against the rock ceiling.

I grab the gun I left out and ready, and pulling my pack behind me, crawl out through the dirt and rocks to the mouth of the cave.

Stars shine in the clear sky, but the moon hasn't risen yet, making visibility poor.

Another gunshot resounds off the ravine wall followed by a pained roar.

Someone is shooting the cats!

I don't know whether to root for them or not. The cats are creatures of such beauty and intelligence, and yet it is most likely that someone is fighting for their life against the ferocious predators.

I hear a noise. Was that a man's voice calling?

"Sample! Watch out!"

I turn in time to see a huge cat jump from a ledge behind me. Its oversized body flies through the air toward me. I raise my gun but realize its trajectory is wrong for an attack. It lands gracefully beside me, and a deafening roar emanates from its wide, tooth-filled maw.

The crack of gunfire fills the ravine, and I jump in front of my cat. Agony flares through my leg. A cut off roar informs me that my cat has been hit as well.

Ignoring my own pain, I kneel down beside the collapsed beast. Blood is seeping from its shoulder.

"No, you're going to be okay." I apply pressure to the wound. The large cat growls and nips at my hand. I rummage through my pack looking for my knife. Liam would kill me if he saw how disorganized my bag is. I growl. Why do my thoughts always have to turn to him?

A battle of roars, gunfire, and yelling is going on around me, but I shut the noise out. All I can think about is the large cat beside me.

"Be strong, big girl," I say, though I'm unsure what sex the cat is. "This is going to hurt."

I place my hand firmly next to the wound. The beast moves its head around, and a large, lolling tongue rasps over my fingers. "Atta girl," I say, forcing myself not to jerk away. As I push the knife into the bullet hole, my cat starts to growl again. It watches my hands with menacing eyes but makes no move to stop me from doing what I'm doing. I push the knife in deeper and quickly dig the bullet out.

The cat roars straight in my face. The sheer volume knocks me back. My breath is coming in fast, fearful rasps, but I move forward again and begin cleaning away the blood. I pull my shirt from my already healing arm and use some of my precious water to wet it. Then, I gently wipe away the last of the blood. More blood flows out quickly replacing it, and I hurry to glue the hole closed. The cat sniffs at the glue and sticks his head out to lick it. I push its head away. "Leave it to dry." He doesn't listen but continues trying to lick it. I shuffle around and force the animal's head onto my lap, creating a barrier between its mouth and the wound.

My own leg is a searing agony. I probably should attend to that as well, but the bullet has exited out the back. I'm confident I'll heal in time. I hastily wrap my blood-soaked shirt around the wound in my leg to stem the blood flow. I'm not paying much attention to what I'm doing though.

The battle has moved farther away. There are more roars and yelling and fewer gunshots. How many of the huge beasts are out there? It sounds like a lot more than the nine that watched me leave yesterday. It sounds like the humans are running low on bullets by how few are getting shot now.

I gently push my cat's heavy head from my lap, and, ignoring the pain in my leg, climb to my feet. I hobble toward the sound of the battle. I don't want the cats hurt, but I really don't want anyone to be eaten either. Fortunately, I don't have to go far to reach the beasts. Even the twenty meters I hobble has tears streaming down my face and whimpers escaping me every time I place my foot down. Pain stabs through my entire leg.

The cats are circled around some boulders where a small group of people stand silhouetted against the star-filled sky, making their last stand.

One of the beasts leaps forward and would easily reach the top of the closest boulder, but a bullet knocks it to the ground.

"No!" I yell. But it's too late. The cat falls dead at the bottom of the boulder. "Stop!" I yell again, whether to the people who are killing the beautiful cats, or at the fierce predators that will surely kill them eventually, I'm not sure.

I step forward, inside the ring of beasts. They swing their large heads and soulful eyes toward me. Some of them growl; all of them look terrifying.

A large cat steps out from their ranks. My cat has followed me and now stands by my side. I breathe a sigh of relief.

The beasts watch me. What do I do now? It seems irreverent to make a shooing motion at them, and I'm pretty confident it wouldn't work anyway.

"Sample, what are you doing?" A fearful voice asks me from the top of the boulders. A voice I know. A voice I know too well.

"What are you doing here? You could have gotten yourself killed! You can't mess with these beasts!" I yell. There's so much I want to yell at him about, but that seems like a good place to start. "It's not enough for you to bully people smaller than you, you've got to come out here and kill these beautiful creatures!"

Liam doesn't answer, and the moon has risen enough to reveal his gaping mouth as he registers my words.

The cat beside me starts to growl, and I realize my mistake.

"Sample get up here," Liam orders.

"I'm safer down here than you are up there," I retort, making an effort to keep my tone more level.

Liam doesn't answer. He's staring at the bandage wrapped around my leg. "Cover me," he orders someone behind him and then he's leaping to the ground beside me.

"No!" I yell, but it's too late. My cat has pinned him to the ground and is roaring in Liam's face.

I throw myself over my cat, draping my body over it to protect it from bullets, while at the same time wrapping my arms around its neck and pulling back with all my might. I don't have the strength to move the beast an inch, but it seems to understand my intent. It moves off Liam, but I notice it's very careful to keep itself inserted between me and the large soldier—as if protecting me. In the same way, I'm standing between it and the shooters atop the boulder.

"Don't shoot, please, don't shoot," I plead. I consider ordering them to put down their guns, but that's probably asking a bit much considering the ring of predators surrounding them.

Chapter 8

I take a deep breath. Animals are growling on one side of me while fingers twitch on the guns above me. I can't understand what Liam and the others are doing here so far from our cave, and more importantly, I have no idea how we're going to escape.

I look to the cat beside me and realize my hand is resting in the thick fur on the back of its neck. Its eyes are locked on Liam. I recognize that look. I had it trained on me for enough of yesterday. It's the gaze of a hunter.

"How are we going to get out of this, hey buddy?" I ask.

"I have a couple of ideas," Liam replies.

"I wasn't talking to you," I growl at the same time as a low rumble emanates from my cat.

"She doesn't want you to talk either," I can't help but smile. It feels good to have an ally who is bigger than the man who towers over everyone else.

"Sample, what are you doing?"

I ignore his question.

Looking around, I ask, "How many did you kill?"

"I didn't kill any," he replies.

"What? You missed?" I scoff. As if.

He holds up his gun, and the cat beside me bunches its muscles, ready to pounce.

I grab a fist full of fur and pull. The cat stills, but I can feel it's ready to move, and I know there's no way I'm strong enough to hold it back.

"Stun bullets," says Liam, waving his gun at me. "I think the others may have killed a couple though. We lost Bobby."

"No," I whisper. Why? What are they doing here?

"Chances are, none of us will get out of here alive." I look up at Brody's familiar voice. My eyes drift to Adam beside him. I can't make out who's behind him in the dim light, but I dread to think how many of my friends have gotten themselves into this mess.

Turning my back on them, I face the beasts around us. I can't let them die. I have to find a way out of here.

I wonder if I can get the animals to follow me. "Come on buddy," I say to my cat, and start to walk toward the ring of large beasts. Every muscle in my body is tensed as I walk away from Liam, leaving him unprotected.

My cat joins my side, and we walk between the beasts together. They've started growling louder, and I want to run back to Liam's side to protect him, but I force myself to keep walking. None of the huge cats try to stop me from leaving, but will they follow? "Come on girl, are you in charge of this crew or what?" She rubs her head against my hand but makes no other response.

We get through the ring and, to my great relief, the cats start turning to follow us away.

When I've gone about fifteen meters, I turn to tell Liam to flee as soon as we're out of sight. The words die in my throat. He's back on top of the boulder, and at least ten cats are advancing on him and the others.

One of the animals throws back its head and roars while another leaps, landing on top of the high boulder. Liam fires, stunning the cat, but another follows. Shots ring out. The beasts roar.

The cats that were following me have turned and are now charging the rock. Some of the large animals fall, but a few have made it to the top of the rock.

My friends are leaping clear. Brody slips and falls. I'm running as fast as I can on my injured leg, but I won't make it to them in time. Brody is trying to rise, but his ankle gives out on him.

A beast leaps at him.

"No!" I scream.

Liam jumps in front of the animal. It flies through the air toward him. Then, my cat is there. It knocks the other cat from its target midflight.

Leaping back to its feet, my cat turns and lets out a deafening roar. I get to its side and reach out my hand to the thick fur on the back of its neck. I don't know why, except that somehow we both seem to be allies in this conflict. It roars again, and the beasts cease their attack.

A bullet cracks through the night air. "Stop firing!" I yell. I'm getting angry now. I look around, hoping that another cat hasn't been injured, or worse, killed. But there doesn't seem to be any newly down.

I start to back up toward Liam. "Come on, we're leaving," I say. "No more shooting."

Liam starts to back up beside me. He pulls Brody to his feet. I stop, while they sort themselves out. I don't dare pull my eyes from the predators that, while not advancing, are still growling, showing their long sharp teeth. My cat doesn't watch our slow retreat. She has faced off with her own pack.

I can hear Brody grunting in pain. I hope he hasn't broken anything.

In my peripheral vision, I see Liam sling his gun over his pack and, turning his back on the beasts, get an arm around Brody and help him hobble away.

My stomach clenches and tears threaten. He trusts me that much?

I swallow the sob that threatens and continue to back up. The others are shuffling backward with me, no one else daring to lower their guns or turn their backs on the huge animals.

We retreat slowly, not daring to take our eyes from the beasts and stumbling over rocks frequently. I hope for no more twisted ankles, but mostly I hope that my cat can continue to keep the others at bay. None of them are following so far, and their growls have lessened.

When we've gone about fifty meters, I turn. They let me leave before, and I'm fairly confident my cat can keep them back, though I have no idea why she is.

I rush to Brody's free side. The sky is beginning to lighten, and I can see his face is pale and slick with new sweat. My sweat has already dried in the cool morning air. I wedge my shoulder under his free arm. Even though Liam is on the injured side, Brody still leans heavily on me.

The others have turned around as well, though tight fists clutch their guns and they throw frequent glances over their shoulders. We pick up our speed now that we're walking forward; me and Liam bearing most of Brody's weight.

We're heading back south down the ravine. They've got another thing coming if they think I'm returning to the cave with them, but I can't leave them now. Not with Brody injured and the cats still so close.

We reach a bend, and I turn to wish my cat farewell. She's right behind me. At least half the beasts are gone, but there's a handful around her, following us.

"Crut!" says Adam when he notices them.

"Be calm," I order. "They're just following us. They did this to me yesterday."

The others have turned around now and quiet but emphatic curses surround me.

"They're not threatening you, so just ignore them," I say.

"Yeah right," says Jake

I had hoped to stop for a quick moment, so someone could check Brody's injury and give him a splint or something, but we need to keep moving.

We walk until the sun comes up. Adam shoulders me out of the way and takes my place supporting Brody. The cats continue to follow us, and we keep going.

"Are they ever going to give up?" asks Carla

I don't know. I thought maybe they had yesterday, but then they were there when I woke, fighting my friends.

"Let's stop," I say.

"Not with them so close," says Ethan

"We need a break. Brody needs to stop. We don't know when they'll stop following us," I reply.

"If they want to catch us, it won't make any difference whether we stop or keep going," Adam agrees.

We find some thigh-high rocks and drop our packs beside them. Liam and Adam lower Brody to the ground. His face is ashen, and I realize he hasn't even the energy to sit, leaning against one of the rocks. I hate that I can't give him any of my energy to heal him.

Dante crouches and, ignoring Brody's cries of protest, rolls up his trouser leg, revealing a hugely swollen ankle. Dante gently probes the swelling, eliciting cries of pain from Brody.

"He's in too much pain and there's too much swelling for me to tell if it's broken. I'll need to reset it if it is ..." he throws a glance over his shoulder to the waiting beasts. "He'll probably scream a lot though…"

As I take a few sips of water, I watch Liam pulling things from his pack. What is he doing here?

Turning my back on him, I wander toward the cats, not questioning why I'd rather be with them than with the handsome soldier I once thought I couldn't live without.

Lips curl at my approach and some of the beasts start to growl. What am I doing? I stop where I am. My cat takes one step forward but doesn't come any closer.

"Why are you following us?" I ask.

She doesn't answer. I hold her eyes for a while until she looks down. The other cats stop growling and a couple of them drop to the ground.

"We need to rest, but it's hard to do that while you're following us." My cat is looking at me again but still refuses to answer me. "You're wasting time Sample," I grumble.

I turn my back on the cats and go back to help the others. Brody wasn't the only one with an injury; I can't let my dislike of Liam drive me away from what I should be doing, as much as I would prefer not to be anywhere near him.

When I get back, I see Liam has crafted a splint from the things he pulled from his pack and is helping Dante attach it to Brody's leg. I look around at the others.

All the old crew who stayed with me at Father Bayle's church are here—Adam, Brody, Conner, Jake, Ethan, and Noah. All except Bobby, I realize with a lump in my throat. Darla, Carla, and Zee are also with them.

"What are you guys doing out here?" I ask. Adam just shakes his head wearily, and I think I detect a note of disgust in the gesture.

I look around at the others. They all look exhausted and pasty-faced. There's blood on most of them. Darla and Zee are crouched over Carla's leg.

"Crut!" says Zee. I move closer. Darla, who is never flustered, is working furiously to push Carla's flesh back together where it's been slashed by cat claws, while Zee smothers it in glue.

"Why didn't you tell us sooner?" Zee demands.

Carla's only reply is to roll her eyes back into her head and collapse backward on to the rock she's leaning against. Her head smacks it with a thud, but she doesn't notice. She's out cold. I reach out with my energy to see if she's still alive, but I can't sense anything. For a moment I freak out, but then I remember she's a clone. Of course, I can't sense her.

Being careful to stay out of Zee and Darla's way, I move around the rock to where I can put my hand to Carla's throat. She still has a pulse but it's incredibly weak. "It's just not working! There's more damaged flesh than whole skin. I can't find anything to stick together!" Zee exclaims.

Tears prick my eyes as I watch Darla and Zee work. I wish there was something I could do. Why can't I heal clones? We're the same as the people in every way. How does my energy recognize the difference? I clench my fists in frustration. If only I knew more about how my healing energy works, but I know next to nothing,only how to let my walls down and put them back up again. I lower them now. Nothing happens. None of my energy leaves me. There are none of the people around for me to heal.

I focus on Carla and her bloody leg. Pushing with all my might, I shove my energy toward her.

Chapter 9

Dominko stood in the middle of the grand ballroom, at least that's what the organizers of the lavish party liked to call it. He did a small circle taking in the stark metal walls adorned with an astonishing number of glass and reflective *ornaments*. He wished he'd brought his sunglasses. It was enough to make a person go blind, even if the lights had been skilfully set to reflect up and away from the high-class partygoers.

A small sigh escaped him. He longed for the ballrooms, he'd read about, in buildings carved from stone and adorned with tapestries and paintings and dancers stepping out together on wooden floors. He glanced at the *dancers* gyrating around him, all caught up in their own meditative trances, barely aware of their partners, if they had any, let alone their neighbors. It was getting increasingly difficult to get a beautiful woman to dance with him. Oh, they were quite happy enough to spend time with him and hang off his arm, that wasn't the problem. The difficulty was that they didn't really even seem to understand the invitation, let alone what to do once he got them out on the floor.

Not that he'd really tried lately. The stunning women batting their eyelashes and baring their skin at him from different corners of the room held little interest to him. Not that any of them would be available to him anymore anyhow. His father had chosen his wife. He knew she was watching him from near the bar where she stood fidgeting with the stem of a white wine glass and wondering whether to follow him out into the middle of the room. She'd followed him to the bar after he didn't return from offering to get her a drink.

Dominko turned his back away from her, refusing to make eye contact and buying himself another minute of freedom. His father's ambition to control him had gone to a whole new level. He was now actively grooming Dominko to take over the business. Dominko didn't know what the rush was; his father was still an active and energetic man. He maintained his health with the same iron fist that he controlled his empire, and he had every advantage that money, science, and medicine could offer. He would live for many years yet. His father would probably outlive him.

Yet, every moment of Dominko's time and every aspect of his life was scheduled. Dominko's days, and most of his nights, were spent at Headquarters following his father around, conversing with businessmen from around the world, and learning about every aspect involved with running the multi-trillion-dollar company. Even this party was compulsory. *It really takes the fun out of a party when you're ordered to be here.* He supposed he could make it fun by doing something outrageous to stir up trouble and embarrass daddy dearest, but what would be the point? His father owned him, and there was no point pretending otherwise. Despite his best efforts, Dominko couldn't quite manage to keep the slump from his shoulders.

A light tap on his arm informed him that his wife-to-be had found the courage to follow him into the middle of the dance floor. He turned around and offered her a wan smile. It was not her fault he didn't want to be with her. She was certainly beautiful, and she wasn't stupid. She'd had the best education money could buy and knew how to follow conversations. No, it wasn't her fault Dominko couldn't summon up his normal charming self.

She put one hand in his and placed the other on his shoulder. His father had even instructed her to get ballroom dancing lessons before he introduced her to Dominko, something not that easy to find anymore. Dominko wondered where his father had scraped up the tutor from. He relented, and taking her in his arms, led her in a waltz. The music had no form or rhythm, so it didn't really matter what dance you chose.

As she began talking, he realized his mistake. He should have chosen a faster and more complex dance; one that didn't allow for conversation. As she continued to tell him about herself, his mind drifted to other things. He couldn't help but think about his genetic engineering project and what his father had done to it. He'd returned home and been unsurprised to find, once again, that all of his computers had been removed. His father must know that Dominko still held all the necessary information in his head, or perhaps he didn't. Dominko had spent most of his life causing everyone, daddy dearest included, to underestimate him.

Regardless, Dominko had had little time, or energy, to contemplate how he would go about restarting the samples without his father's knowledge. By the time he got home each night, he had grabbed something to eat, washed, and fallen into bed. He'd started reading medical journals as a diversion, and he had to admit, they had sucked him in a lot more than he expected. Lately they'd been keeping him awake long past when he should have been putting them down.

"Dominko? Are you listening to me?"

"Uh huh," Dominko replied.

His partner sighed. "Do you want a drink?" she asked, giving up on the dance and conversation.

"Very well," Dominko replied.

They wandered toward one of the bars. After ascertaining her choice of wine, Dominko stepped forward to request their drinks. The service was slower than it should have been, and Dominko found himself, once again, studying his surroundings and the people, all cut from the same mold.

"I don't care what you say, growing organs for surgery is the way we've always done it, and you can't convince me that growing a whole clone for organs is a less expensive way of doing it." Dominko's attention was arrested by the conversation beside him.

"Yes, but, when you grow a clone then you have multiple organs to choose from," Dominko recognized Salvadore's voice.

"Well, there is that. But, the logistics!" His tight business friend, Eugene, answered him.

"What logistics? What is there that can't be overcome? Especially, if we have support in the right places. The City is full of clones that are serving no use and are a drain on resources. Why shouldn't they be put to work?"

"But if the general populace were to find out?"

"I'm convinced most of them wouldn't care at all. If organs and body parts were to be made more accessible at a reasonable price, I believe most honest people would sleep more easily at night."

"That is true, but it's against the law. It would only take a few to raise an outcry, and we could suffer major financial damage."

"You keep thinking along those lines, but why would anyone find out? And anyway, with the backing we have, how could they touch us?"

"Unless he threw us under the bus to save his own hide. It wouldn't be the first time he made someone else take the fall for him, or simply just made an inconvenience disappear."

"We're not just geneticists hidden away in labs. We're in the public eye. He can't just eliminate us."

"Or worse, send us to The City."

Salvadore lowered his voice as if this was somehow more dangerous to talk about than the rest of their conversation had been. "Do you think he really did that?"

"Oh, he did that alright. To his best friend. I'd rather be his enemy than receive that kind of mercy."

Salvadore firmed his voice and attempted to regain control of the conversation. "It's not going to go down that way. You're so determined to look at everything that could go wrong when you should be thinking about how much money we have to gain from this."

"How do you know he'll even back it?"

Dominko turned his head slightly to see them. This seemed like the crux of the matter. He observed a secretive smile play about Salvadore's lips. "Who's to say he isn't already?"

Dominko's head jerked up at that, drawing the attention of the speakers.

He quickly knocked the glasses over that the barman had placed before him.

"Dominko! I didn't see you there!" Salvadore announced.

No, I'm sure you didn't. Dominko plastered a huge grin on his face and swayed. "Salvadore! Hello! And Eugene," He leaned forward and wrapped his wet sleeve around Eugene's shoulders in an awkward hug, leaning heavily on him and almost knocking the smaller man to the ground. "Blasted barman, can't even serve drinks without making a mess!" He swung his arm out in a wide sweep that almost knocked his other neighbor's drink from the counter. "Barman! Replace my drinks!" Dominko yelled with a couple of carefully placed slurs. "How are you fellows doin'?" He asked, looping an arm over Salvadore's shoulders.

"Dominko, you are covered in alcohol," Salvadore protested.

"Well, if not now, then later. It seems inevitable, so why fight it?"

"It doesn't have to be," Eugene mumbled.

"Pardon?" Dominko asked, shoving his face in Eugene's and then pulling away when he remembered his breath wouldn't smell heavily enough of alcohol.

The barman set Dominko's drinks down. Dominko swept them up, did a wide pirouette, causing Salvadore and Eugene to jump out of the way, and left.

He almost walked past Francesca. She reached out a delicate hand and rested it on his arm. "Dominko, whatever is the matter?"

"Nothing petal, let us get some fresh air." She frowned at the uncharacteristic endearment. Up until now, he had been nothing but polite, completely avoiding the flirtatious manner he adopted with his casual dates. But he was feeling flustered. He was quite sure he didn't want to be caught eavesdropping on that particular conversation. He dragged her along behind him toward the closest balcony. When he was almost there, he threw his arm around her shoulders and looked over his shoulder. The two men had moved away from the bar but were still talking to each other without, apparently, another thought for Dominko.

He let out a sigh of relief and took his arm back. They weren't watching him. A small frown creased Francesca's forehead. Dominko wanted to cheer her. He didn't like to make ladies unhappy, not while they were still in his presence, anyway. That normally came later when he refused to see them again. Or, at least, that was the way it used to work. He resisted Francesca though. If she withdrew from the relationship without Dominko doing anything obvious to cause it, then Dominko could escape without blame. He frowned; he suspected she had as little choice in the union as he did.

When they reached the balcony, Francesca seemed to recover from Dominko's strange behavior and began trying to make conversation again. Dominko managed a few noncommittal answers. He really wasn't sure what she was saying, but thankfully they seemed to be enough to satisfy her.

Dominko's mind was reeling from the conversation he'd just overheard. He wasn't sure which bit of information to latch onto first. Dread filled him, more than seemed warranted by the harvesting of clones from The City. He'd busted a harvesting racket before, so he wasn't surprised that people were still exploring those avenues. He was surprised that Salvadore and Eugene would contemplate being involved. He'd always imagined crummy low lives running rackets like that, not leading businessmen from respectable families.

Was this racket linked to the one he busted? Only a couple of security guards had been caught at the time, and they'd refused to give any information about who they were working for. Someone had tipped everyone else off that the enforcers were coming, and they'd all gotten away along with any devices that would have led to the heads.

He was going to need to investigate Salvadore and Eugene. He needed to know more about this. The conversation had left too many unanswered questions. Most importantly, Dominko wanted to know who their big backer was. He was going to need to invest in some more computers. He wondered where he would find the time. He probably should tell his father about what he'd overheard. His gut clenched at the thought. Things hadn't gone well the last time Dominko had told his father about an illegal harvesting racket. If he told this to his father, he might be forbidden to look into it further, and it didn't bear thinking about how Carlos might react if Dominko disobeyed him like he did last time, again. No, Dominko needed more information, and then he would decide what needed to be done.

Chapter 10

I feel my energy leave me and flow toward Carla. It's working! I don't know how, but I'm controlling it!

"What was that?" Darla asks.

"It smelled like mamma Frey's home baking," Zee replies.

They go back to their work, trying to glue Carla's shredded skin back together.

"It's sticking!" Zee exclaims.

"Wasn't the wound worse than this before?" Darla asks.

I force more of my energy toward Carla. My sight goes black and, for a moment I'm not sure which way is up. Strong arms wrap around me, and my sight clears enough for me to realize I'm almost on the ground. Liam's scent accosts me, and a deep sense of longing fills me. I push his arms away and struggle to my feet.

"It's healing," Darla whispers. Sure enough, though still covered in blood, Carla's leg is now mostly whole. Sitting down on a rock and bracing myself with my arm to keep upright, I watch as Zee and Darla clean up Carla's leg. It isn't perfect, but the shallow cuts still remaining should be able to heal on their own now.

"How did you do that?" Liam asks. I ignore him. I wouldn't really know how to explain it anyway.

I look around at the others. I can't see any other serious wounds, though there are a lot of bloody bandages wrapped around different limbs and even Noah's torso. But everyone seems to be eating and resting without too much stress, except for that aimed at the beasts who still watch us.

I push myself to my feet and, swaying, make my way over to Brody.

"Food first," Liam orders from just behind me.

My back stiffens. Why is he following me around and how dare he tell me what to do?

"In case you haven't noticed, we're not at the hideout anymore. I left. And you have no authority over me," I say.

Liam stops in his tracks and, with a feeling of satisfaction, I make it the rest of the way to Brody without him. I collapse beside him. He's lying on the ground with his eyes closed and a sheen of sweat covering his pale, pinched face. Though he doesn't open his eyes at my arrival, I think he's awake. He's obviously in a lot of pain.

I reach out my hand and rest it on his arm. "Old grumpy friend," I murmur. He grunts in reply. I smile. It's not that different to his normal response. My eyes travel down to his bound and splinted leg. My head is pounding. I really should have eaten first, but I can't now. Liam's eyes are still on me.

I open my awareness to my energy well. It's low. I expended a lot more energy on healing Carla than it would have taken to heal a *people*. I smile. But I did it. I healed a clone. Suddenly, I feel like crying. I healed a clone. This is just another proof that we're not different from the people.

I try to sense Brody's wound and what he needs from me, but that isn't something I'm able to do. All I can do is sense my own energy, and I'm learning more about how to control it. I don't have much left but what I have I push toward Brody's leg. My vision starts to blacken around the edges and my brain feels like it's about to burst from my skull, but I shove the last of my energy out of me and toward Brody.

A scream escapes me as pain lances through my whole body. I feel as if I've ripped something deep within me. I fall backward in agony as darkness engulfs me.

I wake to the sound of deep panting and the weight of a heavy furry beast pressed against my side. Pain pounds through my head. What did I do to deserve this? I smile despite the pain. I healed Brody and Carla. I healed clones. They will live, and it is well worth the pain.

Cool night air caresses my face, and yet, my energy levels are still extremely low. I would have expected them to be built up more by now. I open my eyes and slowly sit up. The moon sits high in the cloudless sky, and I can clearly see Brody sleeping beside me and around us both a ring of large cats. Frowning, I look farther afield and meet Liam's eyes.

He's standing about twenty meters away. A few mounds, behind him, look more like resting bodies than rocks.

My stomach rumbles. I'm starving. Looking around for my pack, I discover it a good ten meters away. I groan. I can't walk that far. "Be a good girl and go and get my pack for me, will you?" My cat sits up and licks my face. Her breath is rank and her tongue scratches. "Yuk!" I push her away, and she lowers her heavy head onto my lap.

Brody stirs beside me. "Thank God you're awake," he says.

I want to ask him what's going on, but all that comes out of my mouth is, "Food?"

"Of course," he says, pulling some dried beef from the top of his pack. "Liam said you'd need it."

I curl my nose at his offering. I'm not interested in following Liam's orders. I take the wrapped meat from him grudgingly

89

and stare at it. My stomach hurts from hunger; at least, I hope that's what's causing the pain, but my mouth is dry and sticky, and I don't think I'll be able to swallow the smoked meat, no matter how much I want to.

"Do you have any water?"

He hands me a quarter-full flask. I hope it's not his last one, but regardless, I need the hydration.

I take a few small sips, swishing the water around my mouth, and then hand it back to him.

Tearing the first mouthful of meat requires more energy than I have to spare but as I swallow it down, I already feel a little better. I realize my walls are down.

"Did I heal anyone else while I was unconscious?" I ask around a mouthful of dried meat.

"Everyone," Brody replies.

I nod slowly. That's why I still have no energy.

"How long was I out for?" I ask as I begin building my walls back up again.

"This is the second night."

"Oh no. What's everyone doing for water?"

Brody shrugs.

"And for that matter," I say around another mouthful of food, "What's going on? Why are we here with everyone's packs, surrounded by animals, while the others are over there?"

"I don't really know what happened. One moment I was in agony, the next moment the pain was gone, and the beasts were attacking us again. I sat up to find you on the ground beside me and the animals roaring and chasing everyone away. No one seemed ready for the attack. They just had to run, but before they could mount a defense, the beasts had stopped pursuing them and had created this circle around us. It was really weird. It still is. No one can approach us or go to get their packs or guns. If they come any closer than they are now the animals go into attack mode again. I can't move anywhere, or they start growling at me."

"Have the others any water?" I whisper.

"Yeah, lucky a few of them had their flasks in their hands, so they shared. They, at least, could get out of the sun during the days. You and I just lay here and cooked. Connor and Ethan went out looking for water earlier, but the only water around is that river, and they couldn't get down to it. They wanted Liam to go. They reckoned he could make it with a rope, but he refused to move from his spot. He hasn't slept at all. Just watches us. It's almost creepy, but mostly comforting in some small way, not that he could do anything about these beasts anyway."

I grunt in reply.

"I don't know why they don't just finish us off and be done with it. They have us at their mercy. Maybe they prefer their meat dry," he says.

I crack a smile. I'm feeling better with some food in my stomach and my walls back up. I'd love some more water. My mouth is stinging from the dried meat, but I can wait. "I don't think they want to eat us," I say, pushing myself to my feet. I walk over to my pack and hoist it onto my back. I'd love to take some more time to recover, but we need to find water.

The cat's heads have lifted, and they're watching me with a keen intensity. I ignore them. Brody is watching me too; his face a mixture of alarm and curiosity.

"Come on. It's time to go," I say.

His wide eyes turn to my large cat lounging only a meter from him.

Laughing, I walk back to him and, extending my arm to him, grab his hand and pull him to his feet.

He jumps back as my cat glides to its feet. The beautiful animal ignores him, too intent on stretching out its agile limbs.

"Up." I hear Liam order the sleepers behind him.

Beasts stir all around me. I wind through them, picking up a couple of heavy packs on my way. Brody scurries to stay glued to my side and relieves me of the two packs rather than step away to pick up two of his own. Rolling my eyes and holding back a laugh, I grab another couple of packs and lead the way over to the others.

All the cats are standing now, but most stay where they are. Only my beautiful animal glues itself to my other side. It starts growling as we approach Liam. I can't help smiling as I reach out my hand and rest it on her neck seeking to calm her despite my own roiling emotions. "I know how you feel, girl," I murmur.

Ignoring Liam, I make my way to where the others are now on their feet. Dropping the packs at Adam's feet, I turn to go back and get the others.

"Uhm," Brody clears his throat. "I might just wait here then," he says.

Snorting, I lift my knees and begin to jog. I've been trying to move calmly so as not to alarm the large beasts around us, but we're going to need to pick up our pace if we're to get water before the heat of the day hits tomorrow. I shoot a scowl at Liam as he falls in beside me. My cat roars. I smile in anticipation of Liam's reaction, but he barely flinches. His face the stone mask I've become accustomed to over the last few months; he ignores the animal and me even though he's chosen to jog with me.

Chapter 11

The beasts watch as we gather the rest of the packs and carry them back to the others. We're met with murmurs of gratitude and Conner, quickly followed by the others, pulls a protein bar out. "I'm famished," he says.

"How can you even think about food?" Darla queries quietly eyeing the animals, but I notice she isn't slow to bite into her own bar.

"Let's get water," I say as the others hoist their packs onto their backs. They follow me as I lead the way back the way we fled a couple of nights ago. I grit my teeth. I'm losing so much time it's driving me crazy. I wasted way too much time in the cave waiting. Waiting for Liam to train a fighting force, waiting for Cynthia to wake and send the Resistance with us. Now there is no *us*. Just me. And I'm way too late to get back to The City and prevent the harvesting atrocities on the clones. But I can't be too late. I have to be on time. I have to believe it hasn't begun yet. But I don't even know what I'll do when I get there.

These thoughts circle around in my head as I storm through the chilly night air. I'll tell Finn what is being planned. He can alert the public. Why didn't I think of that before? I don't need the Resistance's help to do that. I know it won't be enough to do more than delay it though. Whoever is behind the harvesting managed to escape the enforcers last time, and we were delivered to Clone Industries. Now their operation is even bigger than before. Finn has nothing more than wild rumors to go on. And really what evidence do I have to offer? The operations will remain well hidden from the public eye, out of sight in The City. I have to find them before I can do anything, and even then, how will Finn get anyone to care?

I'm broken from my thoughts by the drop off before me. We've reached the river. Well, the cliff top above the river. They're hardly the same thing—unfortunately.

"Anyone have a rope?" I ask. Liam begins to unwind the black cord that winds up his forearm. I sigh. I really don't want anything from him. No one moves to pull out any other ropes though, so I guess I'm going to be stuck with the thin cord. I hate using it. Liam has assured me many times—back in the days when we were talking—that it's stronger than any conventional rope, but it still feels too thin to me.

"What length?" he queries. I want to tell him a short length to keep the cord as thick as possible, but there's no point getting to the bottom and not having the length I need.

"If a couple of the guys come down with me and perch on a ledge then I'll need thirty meters," I say, trying to remember how far the smooth part of the cliff reaches above the river.

"Are you sure that will be enough?" Liam asks.

"Thirty-five," I concede. I'll need room to move around and tilt my hands to the water. There's no point just dangling my feet in the water and coming back empty-handed or getting down there and realizing I've underestimated the distance. Liam has taught me some tricks for telling distances, but I'm still not brilliant at it.

"What?" Dante is looking between us with a confused frown. "Liam should go."

I want to growl at him. Why does everyone think Liam is all that? Just because he's a soldier. It's not like that makes him anything special. Just because he's big and strong, with elite training and enhanced just about everything. I catch myself eyeing the way his muscles ripple under his tight shirt.

"Sample's better at climbing," Liam replies with a small smile for me.

I turn away flustered. What was that? I can't be gawking at him! And he can't be smiling at me. We can barely tolerate each other.

"You really want to be the one holding the rope that *he's* swinging from?" I ask Dante. Hoping the comment will offer some excuse for my sizing Liam up.

Liam has already started separating the cord, increasing its length but at the same time decreasing its width. I sigh and try to resist wringing my hands. I know Liam would never let me use it if it weren't perfectly safe. Well, at least, I used to think that. I search his face as he works, wondering if I really know anything about him at all.

When he's happy with the length of the cord, he pulls some hooks from his pack and attaches them to it before coiling most of its length up and attaching it to his belt. Sighing again, I turn away. It was a futile hope that he would let anyone else come down with me. I don't understand the sudden return to his overbearing protectiveness. He hasn't even had a glance to spare me the last couple of months while he's been James' crony. My nose curls. I can't help but hate that guy and the way he bullied anyone who stood in his way in his quest to reach the top. And it disgusts me that Liam stood by his side, carrying out his orders.

Everyone starts handing me their flasks and I attach them to my belt. And then, Liam is approaching me. Before I can stop him, he's hooking the small metal clasp, on the end of his cord, into the purpose-made ring on my belt. His arms reach around me, searching my belt for any weaknesses. I want to shove him away, but I can't move—can't breathe. And yet, even without breathing in, I can still smell him. He hasn't bathed in days, and yet he doesn't smell bad. Not to me. To me, he smells like memories of a better time. He smells like a man who used to fill me with peace while at the same time setting my heart racing. He smells like safety and laughter, compassion and strength. I close my eyes, fighting to hold back the tears that threaten.

And then he's gone. The air around me feels empty, mirroring the hollowness inside me.

I open my eyes to see Liam has moved to the edge of the cliff and is peering down. Screwing up my mouth in disgust with myself I move to his side, ignoring Carla's smirk.

"Uhm, if Sample goes down there and we stay up here, what about them?" Noah asks, gesturing toward the beasts that still watch us.

"They didn't attack you when I was unconscious, you should be right now," I reply.

"But they circled you and kept us away. If they can't follow you..."

"Oh, they can follow me," I cut him off.

"Down there?" Darla asks.

"When I was fleeing them before I found you, I climbed down to escape them. They followed me."

"Down there?" Connor repeats Darla's question.

"Down there," I say, and start lowering myself over the edge.

The climb down is uneventful. I'm attached to Liam by the cord, and I detest the sense of security it gives me. I've made this climb before, only last time I had an arm in agony and predators hunting me. I don't need Liam for this. Well, not for most of the climb, anyway.

When we reach the smooth section, I wait for Liam to find a secure perch. He tests his small ledge and sets his weight so he won't overbalance when he's holding me up. "Come over here so I can recheck your gear," he says.

"You can get over whatever it is that makes you think you can give me orders," I reply.

"Sample," he pleads.

"I can check it myself," I cut him off. I give my belt a cursory check. I can feel it's still secure. I haven't scraped it on the cliff wall much, and the cord is still attached properly.

I move below Liam. The shorter the rope when he takes my full weight, the easier it will be on him. And as much as I'd like to make things difficult for him these days; when my life is hanging in the balance, literally, might not be the best time to do it.

"You ready?" I ask.

"Be careful," he says with a nod.

I scowl at him and, taking a deep breath, let go of the cliff.

I grip the rope with one hand, holding myself in an upright position, and use my other hand and feet to gently push me away from the wall. I don't want to swing too far and unbalance Liam, but I don't want to scrape my face all the way down either.

Liam lets me descend slowly, and I begin to relax, allowing the rope to turn me around so I can peer down at the rushing river, now only about ten meters below me.

"Wow!" I breathe out. Filling the flasks is not going to be an easy job. Water leaps and splashes with force between the two cliff walls.

Before I know it, I'm almost there. "Crap!" I realize the rope is attached to the front of my belt, but I need it at the back. How am I supposed to reach the water?

Liam is still lowering me, and I lift my feet to keep them dry.

"Hold up!" I yell. He continues to lower me, and for one horrible moment, I wonder if I've made a dreadful mistake. What's to stop Liam from dropping me into the river right now? Maybe that's why he's here. Maybe James ordered him to kill me. But even as I think it, I realize it's a ridiculous notion. If Liam was going to kill me, why go to all this hassle? Why check my belt so thoroughly? Why not just attach it wrong in the first place? Because the others were watching. Maybe that's why he wanted to check it a second time; so he could sabotage it.

But Liam wouldn't kill me, couldn't kill me. Could he?

I realize I've stopped descending. I look up at Liam. He's leaning back, balancing his weight against mine, but he's watching me with a confused look on his face. Probably wondering what the heck I'm doing just hanging here when I'm supposed to be getting water.

I let go of the rope and swing till I'm hanging parallel over the river. I'm facing the sky. I press my lips together and give Liam a challenging stare. *Didn't think of this, did you Mr. Know-It-All?* I'm tempted to make him haul me back up and reattach the cord to the back of my belt. But despite my dislike of him, I don't want to do that to him. I'm pretty sure he'd have the stamina for it, but there will still be the climb back up afterward.

Unveiled

I unhook one of the flasks from my belt, and, grabbing the rope with one hand, pull up creating enough slack for me to twist my body and lower the flask toward the river. Liam lowers me a bit farther until I can submerge the canister in the gushing torrent. I'm grateful for Liam's keen eyesight that allows him to judge the distance so accurately.

Even so, waves splash up drenching me to my shoulder, and the fast current threatens to rip the canister from my grasp.

When I judge it full, I pull it back and do the same with the next flask. I keep my feet flat against the cliff, seeking to steady myself from the force of the waves that come at me from different angles. I wouldn't be able to fill the flasks if I was any higher but I'm getting drenched by the wild river, and every wall of water that comes at me threatens to send me spinning.

I keep filling the flasks, being careful not to drop them. My hands are wet, icy cold, and slippery. My whole body is shaking, but I don't know if it's from the cold or the exertion of trying to pull myself up and twist myself around constantly or the fact that every muscle is tense trying to keep myself steady with my feet against the wall.

I'm on the last flask when an even larger wave hits me. The flask slips from my fingers. I lunge for it, and my feet come away from the wall. I go into a wild spin. Grabbing the cord with both hands, I try to steady myself, but another large wave hits me and slams me head first into the wall. Water fills my mouth as another wave hits. My head pounds and I can't breathe.

I'm not holding the rope anymore. I can't even feel it's comforting tug on my belt. I flounder with my arms trying to get above the waves that are spinning me in every direction. My eyes are full of water, and I can't get my bearings.

Feeling air on my face, I gulp for breath but just start coughing. Another wave smashes me in the face filling my throat with icy water. The momentum carries me back, slamming my head into the wall again. A sharp pain cracks through my skull and everything goes hazy. Then, nothing.

Chapter 12

Dominko sped his Bedford truck through the shiny streets of Hollowcrest. It didn't handle as well as the sports cars he usually favored so he couldn't go as fast as he liked, despite the powerful engine he'd had installed. It didn't matter; he was delighted in the beast. People stopped to stare at him as he drove past. They had grown used to the occasional glimpse of his flashy red cars, but they'd never seen anything like this.

The Clash rang out over his stereo. That probably had them raising their eyebrows as well. The raw tunes and political questioning were entirely alien to the society he lived in. How he loved it.

He was going on a date with his wife-to-be, and he was determined to have a good time. Daddy dearest had given him an early mark for the occasion, and he was going to make the most of it. He might not be attracted to Francesca, but she was a sight better than his father. Anyone was better company than his father.

He sang along with the song on the stereo, or yelled may be a better way of describing it. It felt good to release some of his pent-up frustration. "If Adolf Hitler were in London today, we'd send a limousine anyway," he sang. He wondered if any of the people staring at him even knew who Adolf Hitler was, or how much he resembled Dominko's father. Dominko laughed at the thought. That was, admittedly, taking it a bit far, but his daddy dearest was undoubtedly a control freak.

He pulled the Bedford to a jerky halt outside Francesca's building. He still wasn't used to the heavy vehicle. He jumped out and ran to the front of her building. He raised his hand to press the com button, but the sensor picked up his chip's signal and opened the door for him. That seemed a bit presumptuous of his father, but it would be ridiculous to keep standing there with the door wide open. It wouldn't close until he went in or left, so he ran up the stairs, taking them three at a time. It was a long way to the penthouse, and he considered stopping to let her know he was on his way up but decided it would be more fun to surprise her.

She greeted him at her door, all elegance and grace. Dominko was disappointed; he'd hoped to catch her not completely ready. *Oh well. I'm here for a good night out,* he reminded himself, gave her a winning smile which she returned with surprise, offered her his arm, which she took with confusion, and headed back toward the stairs.

She glanced at his sweaty armpits. *Hmm, I probably should have considered that.* It wasn't the most appealing way to meet a lady, even if he did intend to change when he got back to his truck. *Truck, Truck.* "I've got a truck," he sang to her.

"Pardon?" She asked, her forehead crinkling in the cute way it did when she was confused.

"You'll see," he grinned. They reached the stairs, and Dominko turned to take them.

"Umm, might we take the elevator?" she asked.

Dominko's smile died. He guessed it was a bit unreasonable to expect her to go all the way down the stairs. He gave in, possibly not as graciously as he might have wished to.

His good humor was restored when they reached his truck. "What is this?" Francesca exclaimed.

"This, my dear, is a Bedford," he said with a sweeping bow.

"I'm supposed to travel in this?"

"This is the height of fashion," Dominko replied.

"I think your fashion sources are different to mine. How am I even to get into it?" Dominko's gallant nature urged him to step forward and help her, but he didn't want to encourage her.

"I'm sure you'll figure it out," he replied as he walked around to the other side of the truck. *Sample never would have had a problem with it.* He couldn't help remembering the time she had insisted he stand on her shoulders so he could climb to the top of a wall. He peeled his sweaty shirt off and absentmindedly reached behind his chair to grab the spare he had put there.

A woman twittered as she walked past and Dominko flexed his muscles. He noticed Francesca admiring his finely chiseled torso. He stepped behind the metal of the cab to hide himself from her view. "It's so hard to not attract women," he mumbled.

"Pardon?" she asked, having achieved the daunting feat of climbing into her seat.

"It's so large to truck lemons," he replied.

"You truck lemons?"

"Of course not," Dominko replied.

After she recovered from her confusion, Francesca talked amiably all the way to the restaurant. Dominko did his best to interject witty comments and act the part of a date who actually wanted to be there. He was pleased to notice she actually seemed to understand and appreciate most of his comments.

He had to admit, his father had actually chosen better than Dominko had done for most of his previous dates. Though, in truth, good conversation skills had never been very high on his list of desired attributes; he'd rarely seen a woman for a second date anyway.

Yes, Francesca was certainly better company than most people. "I've started reading medical journals. The human body is fascinating, isn't it?" He spoke over whatever she had been saying. She looked at him quizzically.

"Do you use that line on all the girls?"

It was an amusing response, and Dominko gave her credit for her wit, but he really did want to talk about what he'd been discovering. Medicine was surprisingly very different to engineering.

"Have you ever considered kidneys," he asked.

She laughed, a sweet tinkling sound of amusement. "Dominko! What a question! Of course I haven't. Who would ever give thought to such a thing?"

Dominko inclined his head for a response. He had no other reply available, nothing he cared to say. Indeed, any interest in maintaining conversation had fled.

Chapter 13

I'm cold. Wind caresses my back; the feeling unwelcome in my wet clothes. My front is warm though. My face cushioned against something hard but strangely comforting. Something sharp is cutting into my arms and legs, and my head feels like it's going to explode. I try to reach up to feel it, but I can't move my arms.

I open my eyes and searing pain arcs through my skull. Slamming them shut, I try to make sense of what I just saw. I try to move my arms and legs out of the uncomfortable position they seem stuck in. Whatever I'm lying against keeps jerking forward in a strange non rhythmic motion. A groan escapes me as another jerk sends a stabbing pain through my head and a round of nausea through my belly.

"Sample?"

Is that Liam?

"Sample? Are you awake?" he asks from just in front of me.

I don't answer. I don't want to talk to him. I don't like talking to him anymore. I thought I'd escaped him. I don't know why he's in my life again.

Another groan escapes me as I jerk forward.

"Don't worry, I'll get you to safety," he says.

What does he mean?

I open my eyes the barest crack, frustrated that I can't use my hand to shield my eyes from the glaring sun. At first, I can't make out anything. There's nothing close by. But then I see the ground. I'm moving at a slow jerking pace parallel to it. What on earth is going on?

I close my eyes again. The strange view is disorienting and makes me want to vomit.

I take a deep breath. My lungs hurt but for some strange reason, it just seems like a great relief to be able to breathe at all. Liam's scent fills my nostrils, and I moan again. How I miss holding him close. Not that it was ever a regular occurrence, except when we were alone trying to survive in the freezing mountains. I allow myself to remember, just for a moment, and I recognize what I'm leaning against—Liam's back.

Now that I know where I am, I can feel his muscles rippling under his shirt as he pulls us forward. Actually, not forward, up.

My eyes fly open, and I don't close them again despite the agony in my head.

We're on the cliff face! Liam has tied my arms and legs around him, and he's climbing the cliff with me on his back.

"Crut!" Terror fills me.

"You're okay," Liam's warm voice seeks to assure me.

"I'm not worried about me. I'm worried about you. What if you fall?"

"Wouldn't that be an area of concern for you too?" He grunts as he pulls us upward.

"Yes. Of course, it would. Untie me. I can climb on my own."

When he doesn't untie me immediately, I begin jerking my arms and legs, struggling to free them.

"You're not helping Sample."

Stopping, I take a deep breath. Okay, maybe pulling us both from the cliff isn't the best idea I've had today.

"Untie me Liam," I say with a warning edge to my tone.

"Are you sure you're okay to climb Sample? You banged your head up pretty bad, and you were unconscious just moments ago."

"I don't need your help."

I'm immediately embarrassed by my words. I would be dead without Liam, washed away unconscious in the river. No one else would have been able to climb up this cliff with me on their back. Thankfully, Liam is silent.

He doesn't untie me though, and I curse his stubbornness. I don't demand it again though. I know any further demands should be accompanied by an apology or, at least, thanks; and I don't feel like giving him either, so I keep my mouth shut.

The truth is, I'm really not sure if I could climb on my own anyway. My head is pounding. My eyes are closed again; my vision is too blurry to make anything out clearly anyway. And the only thing stopping me from throwing up is the knowledge that it would land all over Liam's back and I'd be stuck in it.

His muscular back pressed against me is a comfort. He saved my life again. His scent reminds me of better times. If I could get rid of my headache and the terrifying drop beneath me, I could happily stay here forever.

Liam stops, and I crack my eyes enough to realize he's standing on a small ledge.

"I can probably let you off here, if you really think it's a good idea, Sample."

Crap. Why did I insist on this? I don't know how to backtrack now.

"Sample? Are you still awake?"

I don't answer. I remember when we first met, and I considered feigning weakness so he would carry me. It wasn't an option then, but now it seems it might be the best option. Why have I always felt this way about him? It's most inconvenient.

When I don't answer, Liam begins climbing again, but there seems to be a greater urgency in his movements. "Crut!" he whispers. "Stay with me, my heart, we'll be there soon."

What did he say? The words were muffled against the wall and I'm feeling so disoriented I don't think I heard him properly. I couldn't have.

Liam's body lurches upward, and then we drop. I take a startled breath, but Liam grabs hold of something, and we stop.

"Slow down Liam."

"You're awake?"

Pausing, I wonder how to respond. "I am now, but a fat lot of good that will be if you drop us into the river."

"Sorry, I'll slow down," he says.

"Mmm, thank you," I murmur.

"You're welcome," he whispers, and I wonder what he thinks I'm thanking him for. Possibly more than just slowing down. Maybe he thinks I'm thanking him for saving my life or for carrying me up the cliff. That's way more than I intended to thank him for, but as I embrace his back and let his nearness soothe me, I decide to let him have the thanks anyway. He probably deserves it.

It takes longer to reach the top than I thought it would and I'm feeling guilty about not climbing off Liam's back and making my own way up long before we get there. But I can't bring myself to leave him. His closeness fills a hole in me that's been consuming me these last few months; and in my weakened state, I can't force myself to peel myself away from him. We'll be separated soon enough.

As soon as we reach the cliff edge, hands grab at us pulling us over the top, as if Liam won't make it the last little bit without their help. He collapses into a sitting position with his legs dangling over the cliff. I'm still tied to his back, and anxious hands are untying my arms and legs. As soon as I'm released, I roll away from him and begin rubbing the life back into my aching hands and feet.

Liam collapses onto his back. I frown at his uncharacteristic display of weakness. Perhaps he wore more tired than I realized.

Cries of relief and dismay surround us and hands fuss over me. I try to swat them away, but Dante is persistent. He orders the women back, and I calm as he begins working on the back of my head. Apparently, my wooziness is from loss of blood too, not just a concussion.

The flasks are taken from me, and everyone drinks sparingly. Liam consumes a protein bar, but I just stare absently at the one offered to me. My stomach revolts at the very thought of eating.

"We should head for the road," Adam is saying.

"I agree. We could waste days trying to find any other way to cross that river," says Jake.

"Sample and Liam need to rest," says Dante.

I don't know why they're talking about crossing the river. I still haven't figured out why they're here at all, but I know I'm not going to waste another day resting. I need to get back to The City. Every hour I waste could be countless more lives lost. I'm consumed with guilt for the time I've already wasted over the last few months.

"You guys can do what you want, but I'm not stopping," I say, pushing myself to my feet. I sway unsteadily. Liam is watching me, and I brace myself for his objection, but instead, he steps toward me and wraps his arm around my waist, lending me his support. I frown at him, ready to push him away, but a wave of nausea washes over me, and everything goes black for a moment. I look around, hoping for someone else to lean on, but no one is offering. Brody bends down and picks up my pack as well as his own. I extend an arm for it, but he just shakes his head and leads the way to the edge of the ravine.

It looks like I'm going to be scaling those horrid sandy and rocky slopes again, but I don't complain. That's the way I need to go. I don't know why the others are going this way, but I'll stick with them for now. It's a comfort to have my old friends with me, and truthfully, I'm not feeling completely up to going it alone just at the moment.

Chapter 14

We climb through the mountainous ridges for the next few days. The big cats follow us the whole time; though, as time wears on, their numbers drop away, and they begin to fall farther back. My head pounds constantly, making it difficult for me to think. The others talk among themselves, but I can't seem to focus on anything they're saying. Occasionally, they hand me some food or remind me to drink, but if they try to make conversation with me, I'm not aware of it.

On the fourth morning, I wake with a clear head. The intense pain has left, leaving only a mild headache and the awareness of a sore neck that I hadn't noticed before when my head was hurting more.

I lie, breathing deeply, enjoying the sensation of not being in agony. I've still got my eyes closed, but for the first time in days, I'm aware of my surroundings. I can hear the occasional bird nearby, a roar from one of the cats in the distance, and the terrified squeal of an animal being slaughtered. There's the chirp of morning insects, the caress of cool air on my cheeks, the smell of beans cooking, and the awareness of Liam close by. It's a familiar sensation, and I realize that he hasn't left my side for the last few days.

A sigh escapes me. Why do I want him close? I don't know what his plans are. I don't know why he's here. I don't trust him. And yet … I do. My rational mind can't find one good reason for it, but every fiber of my being trusts him instinctually.

"Come on, let's get out of these mountains. We need to find water today." Adam breaks me from my thoughts, and the others start to stir around me.

I push myself up, relief flooding me that the pain in my head only increases minimally.

"You're feeling better," says Liam.

I flick him a quick glance and then head for the beans. I still feel no need to pretend we're friends.

We move out quickly. Everyone has been drinking sparingly but even so, we are down to the dregs in our flasks, and we're all feeling anxious. The arid ridges hold an occasional sparse, coarse bush but no sign of water. The animals must get their water from somewhere, but none of us have spent time in the wilderness, and we have no idea how to find it. Even Liam's training was farther north in terrain very different to here.

As we descend the last rocky slope to a sparse forest, I sigh in relief. Though there are still plenty of rocks here, there is also the hope of finding water. Something causes me to turn around.

My cat is sitting at the top of the ridge watching me.

"You not coming?" I ask, though I know she can't hear me from there.

It's weird that the creature whose presence filled me with terror only days ago, now makes me sad to lose her. I wave my hand in farewell, and she tilts her head back and lets out a wide-mouthed roar.

I smile for the first time in days. She sure is a magnificent beast.

We trek through the forest for hours without finding water. Liam has finally left my side and is scouting ahead. I barely see him, and when I do, I receive nothing but death stares from him. I can't help but wonder what thoughts are brewing in his head. Even back at the cave as James' right-hand man, he didn't scowl at me like this. Mostly he just ignored me, and I avoided him along with all of James' other cronies. Come to think of it, I avoided pretty much everyone, except the little people; even my old friends. I'm not sure why.

Carla's whistle drifts through the trees, bringing us all to a stop.

"She's found water," Ethan grins.

Adam whistles back and we change direction to head toward her. A lump fills my throat. They whistle to each other like it's second nature now, sending the messages that Liam has taught them. I wonder how much else he's taught them while I was out foraging with the little people. I know he was training a lot of them to fight, but I thought that had been limited mostly to James' cronies. Apparently, he's spent at least a little time training our old friends as well.

It doesn't take long to reach Carla. She stands proudly over a puddle. I can't feel disappointed. Though the water is clouded brown, it's still water. We rush forward to fill our flasks, careful not to nudge each other and dirty the water further.

"We'll make camp here," Adam announces.

Grinding my teeth, I look around, wondering what to do. There are still a few hours until sundown. I know Adam's decision makes sense; We've been pushing ourselves hard for days and who knows when we'll find water again. If we stop here, we can drink our fill until tomorrow morning and use it for cooking as well. But, the urgency within me, to reach The City and stop the harvesting, is driving me on. I look around at my friends. Am I ready to leave them again? My head is hurting badly after another day of hiking, but I'm fit enough to take care of myself.

"We all need the rest and a decent meal Sample," Dante says, a hint of reproach in his voice as if it's me that's driving them all on.

"Come on Sample. I'm hungry, and I want water," Conner whines. I frown at him. What has that to do with me? I'm not telling the others not to stop. I look around. All eyes are on me. I don't know why my decision needs to affect theirs but the pleading in their eyes is too much for me to resist, so I wander over to a tree and drop my pack against it.

"Yay!" cheers Darla quietly, and everyone starts getting a small camp ready.

Liam is returning through the trees to us. He makes a beeline for me, his face like thunder. Grabbing my elbow, he begins to drag me away from the others. I try to yank my elbow back, but his hand is like a vice.

"We need to talk," he says.

"Give me my arm back," I growl, managing not to show in my voice how much he's hurting me.

He looks down to where his iron fist is clasped around me and winces. He releases me, but the absence of an apology is loud and clear.

I follow him through the trees. I don't know what he wants, but I don't want him manhandling me again.

When we're out of sight of the others, he rounds on me and shouts, "What were you thinking, leaving on your own?" His voice thunders through the woods.

I feel a grin creep up my face. "What was the point of dragging me out here if you're going to yell so loud everyone can hear you anyway?"

All the color drains from his face, and his hands ball into tight fists. The sight of his fury fills me with delight. He deserves a bit of the anger I've been feeling toward him for the last few months.

"How can you be so flippant?" he questions in a low voice.

"I don't know Liam. How would you like me to respond? Am I supposed to cower at your feet like you forced everyone else to do back at the cave?"

His mouth drops open. I wait for him to say something, but he just stares at me.

I blow out a long breath and peer around through the trees.

"I'm bored with this conversation, and I'm tired and hungry. I'm not sure why we're out here having this lovely chat, but I can think of at least ten things I'd rather be doing right now," I say.

He turns his back on me and runs his hands through his hair.

"Who are you?" he asks.

"Who am I? Who am I? Who are you?"

He swings back toward me and starts yelling again. "What are you talking about? I'm not the one who ran away in the middle of the night! Who bailed on all our plans! Who could have run into any kind of danger out there! Who did run into danger! Who bailed on all her friends! Who left me behind," his voice cracks on the last word.

I frown at him in confusion.

"What are you talking about? How could I bail on you? You bailed on me months ago! Bailed on everyone who needed you! Instead of using your strength to help those who were being bullied, like the Liam I thought I knew would have, you joined sides with the bully. How could you? How could you do that?" I turn my back on him, trying to hide the tears that are now pouring down my face.

Keeping my back rigid, I fight not to start sobbing. My anger is gone, replaced by only a deep sense of betrayal and loss.

A tree, only a meter in front of me, fills my vision and I study its rough brown and gray bark, seeking not to think—not to feel. I've been fleeing Liam for the last few months, avoiding anyone who reminded me of him, fleeing these feelings.

After a while, I realize Liam hasn't said anything. Sneaking a look over my shoulder, I find him farther away, perched on a small rock. He's watching me as usual, but I don't know how to read the look on his face this time.

Deciding there's nothing left to be said, I head back to the others. He doesn't try to stop me.

Everyone stares at me when I reach them.

"What?" I spit at them. I know I sound childish but, in truth, it's taking all my control not to just pick up my pack and leave. I don't know how any of them can bear to be traveling with Liam at all. Though, I suppose under James' orders they wouldn't have had much of a choice. They must be here to take me back. It's the only thing that makes sense. And that's why they wanted me to stop because they would have had to follow me if I kept going. Either that or tie me up, and I'm sure none of them want to do that. They probably think they can talk me around.

"Sample," Adam ventures.

"I don't want to hear it," I cut him off.

Dinner is the best meal I've had in a week. It's amazing what you can do with dried food with a bit of water. I don't enjoy it though. The tension in the air is suffocating. Liam doesn't return to the camp, for which I'm grateful, but no one else will even look at me, and they're not talking to each other either.

By the time I lay down, every muscle in my body is tense; my neck is hurting worse than it was in the morning and my headache has returned full force. I work my mouth, trying to release some of the tension in my jaw, but it doesn't help. Nevertheless, it doesn't take long for me to fall asleep.

Chapter 15

Dominko almost drove past Francesca's building. He slammed his foot on the brake at the last moment bringing the Bedford to a jerking halt. Staring out the window, he continued his line of thought. There were so many areas in the brain not in use, imagine what people would be capable of if they could access every area of their brains. It was common practice for geneticists to activate brain receptors to cause clones to operate in enhanced ways. That, of course, was what had been done with the soldiers and healing clones to make them regenerate more quickly. *But, what if we could encourage human brains to operate in the same way? Humans would be able to heal themselves.*

A sharp rap against the window beside him startled him. He turned to see a pouting Francesca standing by the car. Fumbling, Dominko turned the ignition off and wound down his window. "What are you doing out here? I was about to come in and get you," he said.

"You're half an hour late, and you've been sitting there with the engine running for ten minutes," she replied.

"Pfft, impossible, I just pulled up." He jumped out of the car and raced around to the other side to open her door for her.

"The traffic was terrible getting here. Every man and his dog are driving around tonight."

"That doesn't even make sense Dominko. Everyone knows dogs don't drive," she said while very pointedly looking up and down the empty street. "You live three blocks away."

Dominko tried disarming her with a broad smile and a careless wave of his hand. He closed the door behind her and rushed back to the driver's seat.

"Okay, you're obviously too smart for me. You've seen through my weak pretense. The truth is, I couldn't pull myself away from the medical journal I'm reading. It's all about the brain …" His voice trailed away when he noticed the stormy expression on her face had worsened instead of softening in understanding.

When Francesca finally spoke, her voice was icy. "You would rather read a medical journal than be with me?"

Dominko wasn't sure how to answer. He was pretty sure that telling her how much he longed to be at home right now continuing his studies, wouldn't be an appropriate response. But seriously, it wasn't like he'd said he was washing his hair. Though come to think of it, he did really enjoy washing his hair.

"Dominko!" Her sharp voice broke him out of the serene image he'd been building of a luxurious bath.

"Yes? Umm. I mean no. I mean, I'd much rather be here with you," he reached out a tentative hand to stroke her arm. "The journal was just something I had to do for work."

She pursed her lips.

"I'm so glad to be here with you and to leave that behind. Did I mention how beautiful you look tonight?"

Her expression softened, and she patted her hair. "Do you really think so?"

"Angelic," he replied. He turned the engine on and pulled out onto the road so he wouldn't have to look at her any longer.

They drove in silence for a while. It didn't take him long for his thoughts to return to what he'd been reading.

"I had no idea just how fascinating the brain is," he said. "I mean I should have realized, of course. I mean, it controls the whole body!"

When Francesca didn't reply, he turned toward her. She was staring out the window, her features set in an icy glare.

Now what was wrong with her? "Don't you think?" he stuttered.

"What I think is that you should take me home and you can return to your *journals*." Her whole sentence was frosty but the way she said the last word made it sound like something a lot less tasteful to Dominko. Nevertheless, he was sorely tempted to take her up on the offer.

"Do you really think so?" he asked.

"I can't believe you're actually considering it!" she screeched.

"No, no I'm not," he replied quickly with a pat for her arm. He forced his eyes back to the road. He'd learned his lesson about not watching the road when he was driving. There wouldn't be a healing clone around to save him if he crashed again. Never would be again, thanks to his father. His hands tightened on the steering wheel. His father, who would be very unimpressed with him if he didn't make this relationship work.

"I was only joking," he said to Francesca. His words held no real feeling, and he couldn't summon a smile to reassure her. He stared at the road ahead and drove them toward the expensive and soulless restaurant she'd requested for the night's outing. He didn't bother to check whether she was appeased; he didn't really care. He would escort her to dinner as he was expected to. He would show up for everything. It would not be his fault if she ended up not liking him enough to marry him.

The restaurant wasn't far, but they hadn't reached it before she decided to forgive him. Dominko wasn't sure why. She'd probably been ordered to make it work as well. She began chatting about how she'd entertained herself for the last few days. Her news about her friends was as detailed and pointless as a gossip column. In fact, given who her friends were, he probably could have read everything she was telling him in half a dozen gossip columns if he had a mind to.

He didn't try very hard to follow what she was saying; she didn't seem to need more than an occasional grunt to keep her satisfied. His thoughts turned to the conversation he'd heard between Eugene and Salvadore the previous weekend. He'd spent most of his spare time since trying to find out everything he could about them. Try as he might, he'd been unable to turn up any, but the usual, dirt on them.

He'd sifted through all their friends and associates. No one stood out as having any more influence or power than the two of them. Dominko was at a loss to know who they'd been referring to as the person they were hoping to back them. The only person with any real influence was his father, but Dominko was sure they couldn't be talking about him.

Daddy dearest would never risk his empire for something with the potential to be so politically damaging. And why would he want to be involved? *Father has always raged against the ineffectiveness of the current organ plants. But raging against a thing is not the same as stepping out and doing something about it.* As Dominko had daily proof with his own dissatisfaction with his father. *But daddy dearest is very different to me. If he wants something...*

And then, there was the money to be made. Dominko's brow furrowed. It couldn't be possible. Dominko's thoughts turned to the camera outages along the wall. His stomach fell. Surely they hadn't already started harvesting. Surely they weren't already sneaking organs through those unlocked and unmonitored gates. *Why did daddy dearest suddenly stop manning the wall and change the whole security system to a less efficient one?*

Dominko didn't hear a word Francesca said for the rest of the evening as his mind whirled in horror. Once started on that trail, more and more things seemed to fall into place and more questions arose. As much as he tried to deny that his father could be involved in something so horrendous, his gut and his mind seemed to be in agreement that he really could.

Chapter 16

I wake to the cheerful sound of birds chirping in the trees and experience a moment of peace, and then the previous evening comes crashing down on me like the rocks and dust in a landslide, burying me under its weight and threatening to cut off my ability to breathe.

I force myself up. Ethan is cooking again. He offers me a tentative smile, but all I can offer him is a glare. How much time are we going to waste here? I can understand the rest of them are in no hurry to get back to James at the cave, but I have somewhere important to be.

I go into the trees to relieve myself and decide to use the extra time to try to find some fresh berries or something. I don't look for long though, I have no idea what is edible or poisonous.

I walk back to the camp. I'm going to grab my pack and head off, whether the others are ready or not. There's no reason for me to wait for them any longer.

When I get there, the others are packed and just about ready to leave. Jake hands me a plate of hot beans in sauce. My belly growls and I decide it would just be childish to refuse the food. I scoff it down, rinse the plate in the, now almost empty, puddle; and then head out with the others. Liam doesn't try speaking to me, for which I'm grateful. He still keeps looking at me though; just furtive glances. He doesn't make eye contact, which admittedly would be hard as I'm refusing to look at him. I'm still not quite sure what to make of his expression though. It's almost a hurt look. Though, I don't know what he's got to complain about. He was the one who dragged me off into the trees and started yelling. Fortunately, he doesn't hang around for long before he goes ahead to scout.

The day's hike is much like the previous dinner. People keep giving me questioning glances, but no one is talking much. Noah walks beside me for a while and looks like he's trying to find something to say, a hard enough job for him under normal conditions, but probably impossible today with the mood I'm in. I have to give him points for trying though, and his presence does go some way toward improving my mood; even though he has come along to try to take me back. I can't help feeling betrayed that the very people I'd hoped would one day assist me in stopping the harvesting, are the ones who would now try to prevent me.

It's midafternoon when Brody breaks the silence. "This has gone on long enough. I always said she should have been told sooner. If he's gonna just keep sulking, then I'll tell her."

"Tell me what?" I ask.

Brody opens his mouth to reply, but Liam materializes at my side. Brody scowls at Liam and then turns away to keep walking.

"Can we talk Sample?" Liam asks; his tone much more conciliatory than on the previous night.

"What about Liam?" I sigh. "Surely there's nothing more to be said."

He looks around at the others and then gestures into the trees. "Please?"

I roll my eyes at him and lead him away from the others.

When we're out of hearing range, he falls into step beside me.

"I thought you knew me better," he says.

Blowing air out through my nose, I reply, "I thought I knew you too, more fool I."

He gives his head a small shake and gently kicks a rock. I'm waiting for another fight and am confused by his quietness.

"Brody and some of the others wanted to tell you when we first started planning, but you were never around. We couldn't get you on your own and then I decided it would be safer for you if you didn't know. James was watching you so closely—just waiting for the smallest opportunity. I thought you knew me better," he almost whines the last. "I thought you would have worked it out, that you would have realized we were planning something. I expected you to get me on my own and demand an explanation, or if you couldn't get to me, because admittedly it would have been virtually impossible, I thought you would have gotten it out of one of the others. I've had almost no contact with them the last month or so—it just wasn't safe. I thought you would have been in the loop by now. I never realized no one had told you."

I roll my eyes at his rambling, "What are you talking about Liam?"

He grabs my shoulders and stares into my eyes. "Sample, it was all a plan. I was never James' man!" He steps away, shaking his head, "How could you believe that of me?"

"What was a plan? What do you mean?"

Liam wanders over to a rock and sits down. "James was taking control of the Resistance no matter what, and woe behold anyone who tried to stand in his way. Carla overhead him talking to a couple of his boys. You were first on his hit

136

list. He was tired of the way you always undermined everything he said, and he thought he could use you to break me. He saw me as a threat to his leadership. But we were only the beginning. Anyone who stood in his way was going down. He wanted that cave, and only his followers would be permitted to share it."

"So, why didn't you tell everyone? Why is he back there still controlling everything?"

"We couldn't. He already had too many loyal followers, and besides, there were the little people to think about."

"Why, what about them?"

"James never wanted them there. He saw them as a drain on our resources and that they would never be any good in a fight. Carla heard him say he was only keeping them alive as hostages. He had a way of poisoning the food. He told his boys that he'd given poison to a select few of his men, but they didn't know who they were. If anything ever happened to him, they were to kill the little people as retribution."

"No one would do that! What would be the point if James was already dead?"

"I'd like to think you're right Sample. But we couldn't take the chance. I'm sure most of them wouldn't, but it would only take one person to poison and kill any number of people. We thought about just guarding the food, but we didn't know who we would be guarding it against, who we could and couldn't trust, and how would we explain it to everyone? There was just too much risk involved."

"So, you just let him get away with it? With taking over the whole place?'

"We considered leaving. We couldn't get rid of him, and we couldn't stop him, but again, there were the little people to be considered."

"Where could you take them?"

"Exactly."

"So, you went undercover?"

"Yes, Sample! I thought that would have been obvious to you from the beginning, even if you didn't know what was going on. How could you think I would act that way?"

"You did act that way. You acted horribly."

"But, I was acting."

"I could never act like that. You were so convincing," my words come out harsher than I intend them to.

"I know Sample," Liam says sadly. "That's why I didn't want you told. Everything you think or feel is plain to see on your face. I knew you couldn't keep our secret."

"And that's a bad thing? That I'm honest? That I don't think one way and act another?"

"No, it's admirable. I wish I could be as transparently honest as you are. It's a beautiful trait. But, if I were like that, I would have been killed a long time before I ever had to deal with James … a long time before I met you. My ability to act, and appear to be what others want me to be, is what kept me alive in the army Sample. Sample, please don't think I'm proud of my actions over the last few months. I did what had to be done to keep people as safe as possible. I needed to get closer to James, to find out where the poison was and anything else he might be planning. I needed to convince him I wasn't a threat to him and to keep his attention away from you. Not an easy task," he smiles at me. "You're not very good at toeing the line."

He reaches out a hand to me, and I let him take my fingers in his. "I missed you so much, and I hated the way you would look at me. It killed me to know you were angry at me. I never realized just how much you had grown to despise me." The hurt in his eyes fills me with guilt, and I refrain from telling him I actually hated him.

"So, did you learn anything?"

"Not where the poison was, no. I'm not sure, now, whether there really is any or not. I did learn a lot about his other plans though and managed to sway his choices. No one died, did they? I can assure you that if I hadn't been in his trust, there would have been deaths."

"Cynthia did," I whisper. Liam winces, and my head jerks up.

"That was James?"

"I don't know," Liam admits. "I think it probably was. He wouldn't tell me about it if it were. He knew I wouldn't approve. But it is exactly what he wanted."

"What will happen to the little people now? Why did you leave them?"

His mouth drops open. "Are you for real?"

I put my hand up to stop him. "You can't put that on me. You didn't need to follow me. Not if it meant leaving the little people unprotected."

"Sample, you're a fool if you think I would ever let you go back to Hollowcrest without me. Everything I've been doing has been to keep you safe." My head jerks up. "And as many others as possible. And to prepare a force to take with us to stop the harvesting. That's what we came here for—to find help. I was maneuvering myself into a position where I would be able to expose James and take control of his men. I already had the backing of Adam and Jake and the other leaders."

I've ruined everything.

"But, the little people," I say in a small voice.

"They've been warned. They're cannier than we initially gave them credit for."

"I could've told you that," I say.

He nods. "We've left some good people behind who'll keep an eye on things. And I've won some of the men, who James thinks are loyal to him, over to my side. They're still in position, and a couple of them have some influence."

"Though, not as much as you,"

"No," he admits.

I sigh. "I'm sorry Liam. I've ruined all your plans, haven't I?"

He sighs and turns away. The lack of a denial makes me feel like crap. How could I have gotten it all so wrong? I want to yell at him for not telling me everything in the beginning, but how can I? I don't know if I could have kept his secret and he would have been in so much danger if James had realized what he was doing. Really, I'm just feeling so guilty that I ever doubted him. After all we've been through together, how could I have thought such bad thoughts about him? I'm still not sure how he could bring himself to do some of the things he did, like when he knocked Adam out. Though, now I see that Adam was probably in on that.

I punch myself in the thigh and fight to hold my tears back. We could be going to The City with a proper fighting force if I had just trusted Liam, but because of me, we only have a handful of people, the Resistance is still under James' control, and the little people aren't safe.

"It's not your fault, Sample. You didn't know what was happening. I should have let them tell you."

I begin to shake my head but can't complete the action as Liam folds me in his arms and pulls me against his chest. I wrap my arms around his waist. His closeness is some comfort. At least he forgives me, even if I don't deserve it. I don't think I can forgive myself.

Chapter 17

The forest is still. Too still. I've grown used to the constant sound of birds and small creatures, but now my skin crawls under the gentle breeze that fails to rustle any of the leaves on the trees around me. I feel a desperate urge to move more quietly and find somewhere to hide.

Liam has stopped and has that still look of concentration that tells me he's listening. Noah and Adam are still talking, but Carla shushes them. They look around in confusion wondering what's going on.

Liam motions for us to stay where we are and heads off the animal trail we've been following. He's still in sight when a loud crack explodes through the still forest.

I'm halfway to Liam when I realize he's still standing. He hasn't been shot. I turn to the others. No one looks injured. They're standing stock still. Only their eyes betray they've heard the same noise as me.

"Hide," Liam orders, shocking me again. He wasn't loud, but what if someone heard him? He gives me a stern look, and I turn back to the others who are already looking around for somewhere we can conceal ourselves.

When I glance back to Liam, he's gone.

I walk to the others. I'm trusting we're safe for the moment or Liam wouldn't have spoken aloud to us.

Trees surround us, none of them growing close enough to each other or wide enough to conceal even one person. There's nowhere along the trail we've come along that suggests itself.

"Come on," says Adam and leads us away from the direction Liam went in. With one last glance over my shoulder at where I last saw Liam, I fall in behind Adam.

Another crack reverberates through the trees. My whole body jerks. I have to force myself to keep following Adam, my eyes scanning the trees for anywhere to hide. Chewing my lip, I tell myself that Liam's okay.

Eventually, we find a small ridge lined with rocks and small boulders. We spread out and find small holes and larger rocks to squeeze behind. I remove my pack from my back, pull out some smoked meat, my flask, a knife, and my gun. I stow my pack behind another rock and then, leaning uncomfortably with my back against my larger rock and my feet uphill, I settle back to wait.

I'm only halfway through the tough, salty meat when another shot rings out. My head jerks to the side. That shot was louder—closer. But what really has me worried, is the direction it came from—the south, back the way we came from before we turned off the track. Surely, we're okay here though. It's a large forest, and we're nowhere near any trails. But we're poorly concealed; anyone passing behind us will see us. I can see two of the others from where I sit, but what are the chances of anyone happening across us?

Even if they do, it's not like we can't protect ourselves. We're armed and trained, and we have a soldier with us. There are not many out there who could pose a threat to us. Their presence is just a shock after days wandering the forest on our own. I just wish I knew how many of them there are.

A hand grips my shoulder, and I stifle a scream. I look up into Liam's green eyes. "Come," he says.

I follow him as he gathers the others. When we're all in an anxious huddle, he begins talking in a low but quick murmur.

"They're soldiers. About ten of them."

My head jerks toward him. I'm more shocked by his loose count than by the fact that they're soldiers. I had sensed danger, but for Liam to come back without definite numbers is disconcerting.

Noticing my look he says, "I couldn't get closer to them without being discovered. They're out on a training exercise and hunting, but some of them happened across our trail.

They know it's fresh and they won't give up on it until they find us."

"Hairy rats knees!" says Connor, speaking for all of us. My thoughts race. Ten soldiers. They're not out here looking for us, but if they happen across a bunch of clones in the forest, then the best we could hope for would be to be taken in. And then what? The penalty for unviables leaving The City is death. Either we die here, or we die there. We can't hope to outrun them, so we'll have to fight them—a bunch of mismatched clones against ten soldiers.

I look into Liam's beautiful eyes, and he stares back. "They're stronger, quicker, better trained, and with more ammunition than us, but we're smarter," he says. "We can outthink them—and we'll have to do it quickly because they'll be here soon."

"What do we do?" asks Connor.

"We should run," says Ethan.

Shaking my head, I reply, "We can't outrun them."

"Then we'll hide," argues Ethan.

I look around at the rocks we chose to hide out in, and then back to Ethan. He knows as well as all of us, there's nowhere to hide.

"If we run we die," Liam says, putting an end to the argument.

"If we face them we'll die," Brody mumbles.

"They'll be here soon," says Jake. "Does anyone have anything helpful to suggest?"

Ethan glares at him but keeps his mouth shut.

"We could climb the trees," says Carla.

"They'll find us there," says Adam.

"I'm not talking about hiding; I'm talking about fighting from there. We'll have a better view of them coming. They won't be able to reach us as quickly, and we can use the leaves as cover."

Brody snorts, "Because leaves are going to stop bullets."

"We can pick some of them off before they get to us!" she glares at Brody.

"One maybe," says Liam, but he's nodding. "The trees are a good idea. We need to stay close to each other though. We won't stand a chance if we don't stick together."

"What are their weaknesses?" Noah asks.

Liam frowns.

"They don't have any," Jake replies.

"A good adversary will always study their opponent to discover their weaknesses. No one expects you to use their strength against them. They are not prepared to defend against that," says Liam.

"That something they taught you in soldier school?" Brody asks.

"No."

Liam rummages through his backpack and begins removing weapons. "Get your stuff. They'll be here soon."

"How do we use their strength, speed, and ammunition against them?" Darla asks.

Liam pauses and stares at her. She squirms under his gaze, but he doesn't even notice.

"He's just thinking," I tell her. She flicks me a thankful glance but, turning back to Liam, she still looks unsure and takes a step back.

"I'll think of something. Find your positions," Liam says.

I scan the trees around me. None of them are great for climbing; their trunks and branches too thin for any measure of safety and the first branches a good leap from the ground. Carla, Jake, and Adam are already up the best ones.

Dante doesn't look like he'll ever make it up to the first branch of the tree he's chosen. I run toward him and offer him a boost. He begins to protest but decides better of it and puts his heavy boot into the palms of my hand.

Liam is just finishing helping Connor up a tree when I turn around. He gestures to a tree in the middle of the others. I can see its strategic advantage. It will keep the group connected and offer a position to help cover the others. It's also leafier than the other trees and while, as Brody pointed out, the leaves won't stop bullets, I should be able to hide fairly effectively. The first branch, however, is an impossible distance from the ground. I give Liam a withering stare.

He gestures. I release a deep sigh toward him, shake my head and then begin running. By the time I reach him, he's turned his back and bent away from me. I leap and run up his back. I step off his shoulders into the air. His hands connect with my feet and propel me upward. I fly through the air, my arms spinning wildly. Reaching out, I grab the branch above me and digging my feet into the rough bark of the tree, pull myself up and onto the branch.

When I look down, Liam has already disappeared, and I can hear the soldiers approaching through the trees. They are obviously very confident that they're not going to meet anyone who's a threat to them out here. They're not even attempting to sneak up on us.

My mind races. How do you use strength, speed, and ammunition against someone? My mind flashes back to the big cats. A landslide would be helpful now, but the small ridge we're at the bottom of doesn't look too promising. The cats would be helpful, but we left them days ago.

I quietly pull my backup guns and knives from my pack and secure them to my body, while keeping a watch for the first of the soldiers to appear. If there 's ten soldiers and we can pick off one before the rest are alerted and if Liam manages to take out three, that leaves six more. How can we possibly hope to defeat six soldiers? Six Liam's? He could take out our whole group on his own, even if he didn't know we were waiting for him. I smother a snort. When would he not know if someone was waiting for him?

I mark the other's positions. They're not very well concealed. I shift around, putting more leaves between me and the approaching soldiers. I still can't see any sign of Liam. I don't think he's climbed a tree.

What to do, what to do, what to do?

With strength comes confidence, maybe even arrogance. They won't be expecting anyone to be able to beat them. They probably won't even expect anyone to challenge them. Before I've realized what I'm doing, I've shoved all my obvious weapons back into my pack and have left it behind in the tree. I'm on the ground and running for the center of the trees my friends are perched in.

I get a glimpse of Adam's horrified face before the first soldier comes into sight.

Chapter 18

Dominko watched Francesca's lips moving. Her makeup had been applied artfully, and a quick appraisal would show her to be quite beautiful, but Dominko wondered what was beneath the makeup. Why did women have to wear so much of it? What were they trying to hide? He wasn't sure what Francesca was talking about, probably fashion again—a subject that once would have held much interest for him. These days he was finding himself more interested in what was within people's bodies than what was on the outside. Not their emotions or psychology—he really couldn't care less about that—as his inability to listen to Francesca's ramblings about her feelings proved. But their organs, their tissues, bones, muscles, blood, cells—therein lay a wealth of entertainment.

He sighed. He wished he could be at home reading more about it now. He needed to get his hands on some cadavers, not sitting here in yet another soulless restaurant on the expensive side of town, where people were more interested in who was seen with who than in anything any of them had to say—his date included. He would have thought she'd be used to being seen with him by now. Everyone knew they were together. Indeed, the news was full of how serious their relationship was becoming and speculation as to when the biggest wedding of the decade would occur.

"Dominko! Look! It's Catherine Darling; she's with Richard Denver! Now, he's a catch," she purred.

Dominko snorted. Richard Denver was worse than Dominko had ever been at leaving a trail of broken hearts behind. Catherine wouldn't be with him for long. Unless of course, his father forced him to settle down, Dominko thought sourly.

"Dominko, turn around so they can see you."

Dominko stared at her, not moving his body a fraction in the direction she indicated.

"Oh, Dominko, you are so obstinate. Catherine, over here," Francesca called. "Now, you see what you've made me do. I really am making quite a scene."

Her feigned horror did nothing to hide her smile of delight as people turned to look at her.

Dominko put his hand over his wrist device as if to cover its vibrating. He tapped the screen and held it up, pretending to read a message.

"Oh no," he moaned.

"What?" Francesca asked as she smiled and waved at Catherine and Richard who were making their way over.

"It's work. There's a security issue that needs my immediate attention."

"What? No. There are others paid to handle that. They don't need you there."

"I'm afraid I am needed. There's no one else able to manage the operating systems as well as I. It really is an emergency, I'm afraid," he said, rising from his seat.

"But, I don't want to go," Francesca whined. "Ten more minutes."

"I wish I could accommodate you, sweetness, but it's out of my control. I can send a car to pick you up later if you like?"

"Oh don't be ridiculous Dominko," she said, shoving her chair back and throwing her cloth napkin down on top of her half eaten meal. "I can't stay here on my own!"

"As you wish," Dominko replied, offering her his arm. "Good evening," he said to Richard and Catherine. He found himself quite able to give them a large, genuine smile as he sailed past them. Francesca tugged on his arm, attempting to stop, but he pulled her forward and toward the fresh night air outside.

He dropped the disappointed Francesca off and drove away in his Bedford. What was he going to do now? He was out, the night was young; he didn't have Francesca on his arm. He beeped his horn a few times in excitement. When did his life become so regulated that a few hours of freedom became precious? He wanted to speed, to feel the air rushing through his hair and a powerful machine responding to his every whim. Unfortunately, he was in the wrong kind of vehicle for that. He'd considered getting a new sports car a few times recently, but Francesca's horror of being seen in the Bedford was enough to make him want to keep using it.

What should he do with his free evening? He couldn't really go anywhere. There would be little chance of it not getting back to Francesca if he did. He didn't feel like going straight home though. His life these days consisted of tailing his father at Headquarters, escorting Francesca on boring dates, and arriving home late from work, or Francesca, to fall asleep with a book in his hands. He wanted, needed, to do something else, but where could he go where he wouldn't be caught out?

I could go and check out security, he mused. He never got to go to the old security building anymore, and his father had, once again, forbidden him to use the labs beneath. He could go and spend a bit of time observing some of his old projects in The City.

Yes, that's what he'd do, he thought as he pushed his foot down on the accelerator.

It felt weird turning up to the dark, locked building. It still baffled him that his father didn't feel the need to maintain even a skeleton crew to watch the wall. He sighed in relief when his chip scan allowed him access to the building. He bounded into the large entry floor and, turning right, made a beeline for the stairs. He raced up them and burst through the door onto the floor of the surveillance cameras. Pausing, he took a deep breath. Ah, the sweet smell of stale sweat, polished metal, and warm silicon. He sauntered across the room enjoying the nostalgia of visiting a place that was as much home to him as his own apartment.

He stopped when he reached his old computer and palmed it on before sitting down. The screen flashed, revealing a red flashing light.

Chapter 19

I huddle in the dirt and, gripping my ankle, cry for all I'm worth. The approaching soldier signals the other soldiers who I can't yet see. I recognize the sign from Liam. 'Target in distress.'

I watch him approach through a curtain of my hair. I haven't been able to work up any real tears so, raising my hand from the dirt, I spit on it behind my hair and, pretending to wipe my eyes, smear my face with dirt. Perhaps if I look like enough of a wreck, they won't notice I haven't really been crying.

The soldier's walk is confident and relaxed. Two of the others are within sight now. I need to get them all here.

He's almost to me when I look up and start. "Crap! Where did you come from?" I cry.

"Take it easy. I'm not even armed."

I look him up and down and shuffle back in apparent fear.

He smiles. "Yeah, well."

"What are you doing out here?" he asks.

"I live out here."

He frowns and then leaning forward, stares at my eyes. "You're a clone!" he exclaims.

I nod slowly. "Are you going to kill me?" I whisper.

He pulls his gun from where it's slung over his shoulder. "What are you doing out here?"

"I've always been out here. I don't remember anything else."

"Hey! Come check this out!" he calls.

Four more soldiers appear from different sides and come to join us.

"She says she's always lived out here."

"Who cares? Shoot her so we can find the others."

"Look at her eyes. I've never seen her type before. Maybe we should take her back."

"It's a killing exercise, not a hostage drill," says another soldier who's come to join us.

"That's for animals, not clones with purple eyes!"

"What difference?"

"See what the others say," the first soldier says.

"You're wasting time. The other teams will beat us if we don't get a move on."

"I found her."

"We're a team!"

"Exactly. So we'll see what the others say."

A whistle pierces the air. The argument has ended, and with nothing else to distract them, they turn their full attention to me. I sniffle and try to look suitably cowed. I clutch my ankle and let out a little whimper.

"Where are your friends?"

"They're hunting. They said they'd come back for me when they've got something. We're hungry," I shrug.

The second guy gives me a disgusted look and, losing interest, turns to look through the trees. A moment later two more soldiers approach. The first soldier looks irritated.

"Where are the others?" he asks.

"Looking for the track; it disappears. What's the holdup?"

"He wants to take her back," the second soldier says.

"Not the mission. Shoot her."

"She's got purple eyes," the first soldier says.

"I said shoot her." His tone leaves little doubt about whether his instructions will be carried out or not.

The second soldier raises his gun. Before he gets it leveled at me the air erupts in a cacophony of gunshots and the soldiers around me fall.

As they hit the ground, they roll and lift their guns toward the trees. All except the first soldier whose gun is leveled at me. I kick out with all my strength, hoping to kick his weapon from his hands. He maintains a good grip on it, but at least it's momentarily aimed away.

That's enough for me to slip my knife from my sleeve and lunge at him. He rights his gun, but I slash his arm.

"Crut!" He exclaims as blood spurts through his sleeve. He drops his gun, but instead of clutching his arm, he lunges for me, face as black as thunder. He's on top of me faster than I can blink. I can hear gunfire repeating around me, but there's nothing I can do for my friends. I kick, knee, and thrust my knife into the soldier, not even thinking to aim for his weak points.

He gets his hands around my neck. He's strong. I can't breathe, but my neck will snap before I run out of air. I thrust my knife and feel it enter up under his ribs. The rage leaves his face and the pressure on my neck releases. He looks at me with eyes full of shock and then collapses onto me.

The handle of my knife is pressing painfully into my chest, and my hand is wedged around it twisting my wrist. My other arm flaps uselessly around his body. Shots still ring through the air. There may be less than before, but it's so loud I can't really tell.

I wriggle my body out from under him, desperate to help my friends. The first thing I see is the second soldier. He's lying beside me, his eyes wide open and multiple bullet holes in his head.

I pull my gun from the back of my trousers and roll over. I see two soldiers crouching below trees and shooting upward. Neither of them are looking my way. I shoot them both in the head before they notice me.

I can't see anyone else, so I risk rising into a crouch. There are two other dead soldiers farther away. They must have been making their way to cover. There's still a lot of gunfire, but with all the shots coming from the branches, I can't pinpoint the remaining soldiers.

A scream catches my attention. I turn to see another soldier fall to the ground from behind a tree. Liam is behind him. He rushes toward me.

"The others?" I ask, looking around.

"Finished," he replies.

I keep searching. What if he didn't find them all? There were at least two not in the clearing.

The tension begins to seep out of my body. If Liam says he got them all, then he did. My eyes dart to the trees. Was anyone killed?

My friends are slowly making their way down. Carla drops from a high branch, lands and rolls, then is on her feet and running. I raise my gun but when I see where she's heading my breath catches in my throat.

Adam is lying on the ground in a pool of blood. I follow Liam toward him at a sprint.

When I get there, Liam is already applying pressure to a wound on Adam's leg. "A bullet must have nicked the main artery," he says. "He's bleeding out."

Adam's face is white, his eyes closed and his breathing shallow. I open my senses and lower my walls. Nothing happens. I concentrate on pushing my energy toward Adam. It leaves me in a rush, and I collapse to the ground.

I struggle for breath, trying to keep conscious. Last time I tried to heal a clone, it was virtually impossible, but this time my energy leaped from me.

I open my eyes. Liam is standing beside Adam.

"Did it work?" I ask, my voice a faint murmur. Liam turns worried eyes on me.

"The wound is closed," he says.

Dante is leaning over Adam now. His fingers pressed to his wrists. Adam is still unconscious and deathly white.

"He's lost too much blood," says Dante.

"But he'll survive," I say.

Dante shrugs. "His pulse is very faint."

I close my eyes and begin to lower my walls again.

"Sample! No!" Liam shakes me, breaking my concentration. "You've given enough of yourself. One day you're going to push yourself too far, and you won't be able to recover."

"Not today," I say, closing my eyes again.

"Then stop!"

"I won't let Adam die!" I yell, pushing him away.

"Sample, please," Liam begs.

I look into his eyes. "Liam, who would I be if I let Adam die? You can't really think I can just sit back when I have the ability to help him."

Liam swallows hard and takes a step back. I try to ignore his worried eyes and, closing mine, concentrate on lowering my walls again. I start slowly, but there's no point. I can feel I'm almost empty. I take them down the entire way. A wave of nausea washes over me as the last of my energy seeps out.

Liam sits down behind me and wraps his arms around me holding me up. I concentrate on his nearness instead of the headache that's pounding in my temples. His goodness and strength comfort me. I can feel his muscles through our clothing, but more than that, I can sense the life pulsing through him. He has so much inner power. Not just health and vigor but wholeness and rightness. His vitality bolsters me, strengthening my weakness; distracting me from the power leaving me. Instead, I focus on Liam's beautiful energy.

My eyes open with a start. Adam is sitting before me, his color returned and breathing normal. My headache is gone, and I feel strong. Liam's arms fall away from me, and I twist around to see him white-faced, holding himself up with his arms behind him.

"Liam! What's wrong?" I ask.

"Nothing," he shakes his head and then winces. "I'll be fine." His voice is gruff.

"You're not fine! What happened?" I scramble around him, searching his body for a wound. "Were you shot?"

He laughs, grabbing my arms and falling onto his back.

Alarm bells go off in my head. Even his laugh sounds weary but worse than that is the fact that he's allowed himself to lie down when there could still be danger nearby.

"What is wrong with you?" I yell as I push myself up.

"Sample," Dante's soft voice cuts across my panic.

I turn to him.

"I think you may have drained him."

Chapter 20

"What? I can't do that. I don't drain people." My eyes turn to Liam who, despite his obvious exhaustion, is glaring at Dante.

"No," I say, turning to Adam who's now standing, looking perfectly healthy. My hands run over my body. I have none of the aches or pains I should have. My head is fine. I turn away from them and check my energy reserves. I'm half full!

"What did you do?" I yell, swatting Liam's arm.

"It wasn't me Sample." He's lying on the ground with his eyes closed. He doesn't even try to stop me from hitting him.

"You must have done something."

"I held you. That's it."

I want to sit in the dirt beside him and contemplate what just happened, but I haven't checked on the others yet, and I don't feel safe here with other soldier teams out, especially with Liam lying on the ground instead of scouting.

Standing up, I turn my back on Liam. "Where are Carla and Jake?" I ask.

"Scouting," Dante replies.

"Is anyone else hurt?"

I follow Dante's eyes to where the others sit nearby.

"Are they okay? Who's hurt?"

"There's nothing too serious," Dante replies.

"What does that mean?" I ask, following him toward them.

"Who's hurt?" I ask when I get there.

Darla nods toward Noah, and I notice his blood-soaked trousers. The sight reminds me of Adam's injury. Hands shaking, I rush toward him and drop to my knees beside him.

He's sitting up, his face pinched in pain, but at least he's conscious. I can see his leg has been bandaged under his trousers. The wound is in his calf, not his thigh.

"I've got the bullet out. As long as it doesn't get infected it will heal with time. He won't be able to walk on it for a bit, though," says Dante.

I shake my head and begin to lower my walls.

"Sample. You've used enough of your energy today. It can wait," says Dante.

"There are other teams of soldiers around. He needs to be able to walk," I reply.

He sighs, then sticks out his arm. "Use my energy then," he says, grasping my hand.

"No!" I jerk my hand away, recoiling in shock.

"There are other soldiers around. You need to be able to walk," he mimics me.

My jaw drops. Where is this coming from? Dante never acts like this.

"I will be able to walk," I reply.

"Last time you used all your energy, we were stranded for days surrounded by terrifying beasts. We can't run or fight while carrying you Sample."

"I'm engineered to rejuvenate. I don't even know what will happen to you if I use your energy."

"Well, just use a bit."

"I don't know how. I don't even know how to take it. I didn't even know I was taking Liam's and look at him! If I wiped him out, who knows what I'll do to you?"

"Sample, we're heading into an impossible fight. There are going to be more injuries. You won't be able to heal all of us on your own. If you don't learn this now, people will die," says Darla. Her calm voice helps me to focus. I stare into her eyes. I've never met anyone as brave as Darla. She's never afraid to try something new even if she isn't as physically capable as some of the others. She never lets that stop her, and she never loses her cool.

"You should learn this now Sample, while you can," adds Connor.

Dante reaches his hand to me again. I take it tentatively. "I really don't know what to do," I say.

He cracks a smile. "Don't worry about it. You can always heal me if you need to."

I should have done that for Liam. My eyes flick to him, but he's already sitting up chewing on some dried meat. At least he rejuvenates quickly. I will need to be much more careful with Dante.

I close my eyes and begin to edge my walls down. My energy glides over the top and into Dante. I edge them up again with a smile. Well, that didn't work. It seems like my body's instinct to only heal the people is totally gone. Somewhere along the way, I seem to have completely broken the block.

"Crap!" Dante exclaims. "That went backward! All my aches and weariness are gone!"

I laugh out loud.

"Try again," says Darla.

"I need to save my energy for Noah," I protest.

"Dante is healed now. You won't lose any more to him. This is something you need to get a handle on now, Sample." Liam has come up behind me. My shoulders slump. I'm not going to get out of this without a major argument. I try anyway.

"There are more soldier crews around."

"The closest will be at least a half day from here, but we need you both at full strength. Which means you must learn to use other's strength."

I shake my head and look around. There's no one on my side. Everyone's eyes are on me.

"We need you Sample," Connor says.

A frown creases my forehead. This is something they want me to do to help them? But it feels the complete opposite. Everything in me revolts from the idea of taking other people's energy. Darla's steadfast eyes bore into me, Carla's are full of understanding, Brody's are demanding, Dante's pleading, Noah's are just full of pain. But they all want the same thing from me.

I can't stand Noah's agony any longer. I desperately want to heal him immediately, but instead, I turn to Dante, take his hand again and, concentrating on its warmth, try to pull his energy from him.

Nothing happens.

"It's not working," I say.

"Seriously, Sample. I saw how long it took you to learn how to lower your walls slowly. You've got to want this to achieve it. You can't just give up straight away. You'll be able to help so many more people if you master this," says Liam.

His words spark my interest. Imagine how many people I could heal if I could just harness a little bit of energy from a city full of people.

I focus again on Dante's hand, trying to recreate what I did with Liam. I feel my cheeks redden. I can't think of Dante in that way. Pushing my embarrassment away, I concentrate on the strength in Dante's hand. I feel for his energy, and to my surprise, it's right there; simmering just under the surface. I pull at it, and this time, as I'm concentrating on what I'm doing, I feel it rush to me. I let go of his hand and jump back as Dante falls to the ground.

"Is he okay?" I exclaim.

Carla is already leaning over him holding his wrist. "His pulse is strong," she replies. "You didn't take too much."

"I did if he's unconscious! Now he's the one who can't run and fight!"

"It was your first attempt," Darla replies. "You did well."

I shake my head. "I can give him some back," I say, stepping toward him.

"Sample, no. There are others injured who need it more," says Liam with his hand holding my arm back.

"What? Who?"

He nods toward Brody, Ethan, and Zee. I run the few steps to them. "What's wrong with you?" I exclaim.

"Nothing serious," Brody says, waving me back. "See to Noah first."

I take a deep breath and walk back to Noah. My eyes flick to Dante, still lying unconscious on the ground. It feels wrong to do this with his energy, but he's a nurse. I know he would want it.

I lower my walls and let Dante's energy seep out and heal Noah. When I think I've given him enough, I direct the energy toward the three behind me. Their sighs of relief tell me they're better.

Opening my eyes, I see the color has returned to Noah's face, and the pinched pain lines around his eyes are gone.

"Everyone all better?" I ask.

A chorus of 'yes' and 'thank you' surround me. "You did great, Sample," Connor says. The praise surprises me. This is what I was engineered for. I don't need to be praised for it.

Dante is the one who should get the praise. He risked everything. I had no idea what I was doing and could easily have completely depleted him. I check my energy. It's back at half again. "It was all Dante's energy, I say. I didn't use any of mine."

Liam grabs my arm again as if he knows what I'm going to do. I ignore him and lower my walls, giving Dante half my energy, taking my levels down to a quarter. A pounding headache falls on me like a boulder. But as Dante sits up groggily asking if it worked, I can only smile.

Chapter 21

Dominko's gut clenched. Another camera down. He stared at the blinking dot on the computer before him, every muscle in his body tense. His mind, like his body, paralyzed.

He slumped back in his chair. "I should have stopped tormenting Francesca and bought a new sports car," he announced to the empty room. "Then I'd be speeding around the streets of Hollowcrest, like I should be, instead of heading off into danger." He stared at the blinking dot a moment longer before clenching his fist and rising from his chair with determination.

As he ran back down the stairs, his mind raced. What was he to do about a car? He couldn't check out a sedan at this time of night without inviting questions, and he couldn't leave the Bedford anywhere near the outed camera. Someone was bound to notice it on the wrong side of town.

He arrived back at his apartment a ball of frantic energy. He changed into his jogging gear and dug to the bottom of his cupboard for an old blonde wig. It wasn't much, but sunglasses would look suspicious at this time of night, and a scarf would just be ridiculous at this time of year.

He stopped briefly in front of the mirror to position the wig. Once in place, he pushed the suction clip and it firmly attached to his scalp. He gave himself a quick appraisal. He was clearly recognizable if anyone chose to look closely.

Well, he hoped not to be seen by anyone anyhow so it would have to be good enough.

Dominko parked around the corner from the busy nightclub he used to frequent. If anyone noticed his car here, they would wonder why he hadn't used the valet, but he could easily explain that away as his not wanting to be seen without Francesca. Indeed, if anyone asked about his being here, he would just deny it. No one would believe him of course; there was only one Bedford in Hollowcrest, but he wouldn't have to explain why no one had seen him inside if he denied ever being here.

He would much prefer the trouble he'd get from daddy dearest and Francesca for ditching her for the night than the trouble he might find if his father knew what he was really up to—especially if his suspicions were right.

Dominko sat in his car until the street was empty then leaped out and raced away from the nightclub toward the

Melina Grace

train stop. His device informed him there was a train due in two minutes. He picked up his pace.

He could hear the train approaching as he turned the corner. For the first time, perhaps in his life, he wished there was a train line near his apartment. Then he could have timed this better and not had to worry about leaving his truck out for anyone to see.

He reached the stop just as the train was about to leave. He slipped in as the doors were closing.

"Just made that," an old guy commented.

Dominko gave him a wave over his shoulder and walked in the other direction. He couldn't remember the last time he'd ridden a train. He eyed the booths, wondering how sanitary they were. Choosing one at the far end of the carriage, he tried not to cringe as he slid into a seat. He would have preferred to remain standing, but he was hidden from casual observation here.

He sat stiffly, trying not to touch anything for the seven stops until he reached his destination.

Dominko peered around the corner toward the wall and the door with the camera outage. He tapped a nervous hand against his thigh. He dreaded to think what he might find.

176

Nothing was there. The door was closed, and the night was quiet. Instead of feeling relieved, his fear heightened. Now he was going to have to investigate, and that would be a lot riskier than just peering around a building.

Taking a deep breath, he raced for the door. The red light that would indicate the camera was operational was out. Dominko pushed on the door, and it opened. He stuck his head through. Everything was quiet on the other side. He stepped through and pulled the door closed behind him.

His heartbeat quickened. Up until now, he could have claimed he was just checking out the broken camera, but there was no explanation he could give as to why he was on the wrong side of the wall. He wasn't sure if he was more terrified of what the unviables might do to him or what his father could do to him. Dominko had a sneaking suspicion there was something wrong with that.

He crossed the street; he was way too conspicuous standing out in the open by the door in the wall.

Crouching in the shadows by an old, large stairway, he stared back at the unlocked door. He knew he should be terrified by the fact that any unviable could just walk through there and make their way undetected into Hollowcrest, but he found himself more concerned about the evil that might have found its way out of Hollowcrest and into The City.

He looked around, searching for inspiration. The street was empty. He hadn't stopped to think about what he would do once he got here. Belatedly, he realized, he would have been better off using the surveillance cameras to find out if anything suspicious was happening, rather than coming here himself.

But that wouldn't have worked. If there was harvesting happening in The City, then the person who was shorting the system for the door and camera at the wall would also make sure there was no camera surveillance of what they were doing here.

That was it! Dominko wracked his memory, trying to remember what places didn't have surveillance. There were a few. Unless a subject of significant scientific interest moved to a place where the cameras had outed, his father hadn't authorized the expense of repairs. There was only one place that had gone dark in the last year though.

A fresh wave of fear seized Dominko. It was in one of the worst parts of The City with the cruelest and most dangerous gangs. *I should just go home and tell the enforcers about my suspicions.*

Dominko shook his head. That's all he had—suspicions. Nothing the enforcers could act on, and even if they could, they had neither the authority nor the people power to infiltrate The City.

Dominko smothered a snort. As if he had the people power. Well, he would just have to be stealthy. At least he'd worn sneakers this time. He started running down the street.

Chapter 22

I move through the trees as quietly as I can, careful to keep Liam in my sights and trusting the three spread out behind me to keep sight of me. I hope we're not more likely to be seen spread out. Liam is sure, however, that we have a better chance of escaping notice this way and we're more likely to discover the enemy more quickly. Basically, we're all scouting instead of relying on just a few to scout for the rest of us.

The birdsong that fills the trees is soothing. At least I know there's no one hunting close by at the moment. As long as that remains the soldier's brief, we should have plenty of warning before we meet them.

I try not to stare at Liam's back too much. I'm supposed to be watching the trees for any sign of soldiers. I glance around and let the peace of the forest wash over me. My eyes quickly return to Liam. Even at this distance his strength and grace are obvious.

A torrent of emotions threaten to engulf me. I had thought I hated him, thought I'd left him behind and would never see him again, believed I'd been mistaken about who I thought he was, that he wasn't the man I'd hoped he was.

But he is, all that and more. I'm still finding it hard to believe he followed me. Left all his plans and hard-won ground to come after me. But why? He's always sought to protect me for some reason, ever since he first shot me with a paralyzing bullet back in The City. He's turned his whole life upside down more than once to follow and protect me.

I don't know what it means. I know what I want it to mean, but he's never so much as tried to kiss me. Surely with all the time we've had together, he would have kissed me if he wanted to. Maybe he thinks of me like a sister or something. Actually, that would explain all his behavior.

The thought is crushing. I bite my lip, trying to hold back tears. I look around at the trees again, but there's no solace to be found there.

A shrill whistle pierces the air. "Crut!" Liam told us not to use the whistle signals as any soldier would realize they weren't a natural part of the local fauna even if we did try to adapt them. If Carla is whistling, then we must already be discovered, or at least she is, and she's trying to warn us away.

Liam is gesturing frantically for us all to join him. I race toward him. When I get there, he puts his hands out to boost me upward.

"Get up the tree and see what you can see," he says. I take his boost, and he throws me upward. I grab the lowest branch and pull myself up. I scramble from branch to branch, the trunk and limbs getting dangerously thin. I keep my feet wedged in the crook between branch and trunk where they're the strongest. The trunk still sways unnervingly with my weight. No matter how high I climb, I can't see anything—just branches and leaves of other trees.

I look down, making eye contact with Liam's questioning gaze. I shake my head and then try to climb a bit higher.

I can still hear his quiet voice, even at this height, and I wonder how far it's traveling through the trees.

"You all head north-east away from this crew, and I will go and free Carla," he's telling them.

I take one last look around. Seeing nothing, I begin to slide down the tree from one limb to the next. The bark is smooth, but my hands still manage to catch on countless nobs and sticking out bits, taking the skin from my palms and gouging more than one sore into my fingers. I ignore the pain. This is one conversation I'm not missing out on.

I leap from the last branch and land beside Adam.

"Like hell," he's saying. The others are all shaking their heads.

"You can't take on a crew of soldiers on your own Liam, and we won't leave Carla behind," Zee says.

Looking down at my bleeding hands, I sigh in regret. I needn't have rushed quite so much. I lift my chin and smile at Liam. He rolls his eyes at me.

"Is it too much to ask that you support me in just one thing?" he asks.

"Definitely," I reply.

"Fine then. Find somewhere to hide. Somewhere better than last time. I'll come back when I've checked out the situation."

He sprints off into the trees without waiting for any more arguments. We look around at each other. I don't know about the others, but I'm wondering if it's even worth moving from where we are. We've been walking for two days since our last encounter and haven't seen anywhere that would be decent to hide.

"We could just climb trees again," suggests Zee.

"You and your bloody trees," complains Brody, but we all fan out and look for some good ones. We choose a few larger ones that aren't spaced too far apart and help each other up until only I'm left on the ground. I choose a tree that's not too difficult and am soon hidden behind as much foliage as I can be.

We wait.

An eerie silence fills the forest. All the animals have left or gone into hiding. I'm not sure what scared them away. There are no gunshots or any sign of hunting soldiers. Nothing but an oppressive silence that weighs me down demanding that I run as well.

I fight not to tap my fingers. I know how sharp Liam's senses are and can only expect the other soldiers to be as enhanced. I release a long quiet sigh. Where is Liam? He's probably taking them all on by himself and will be back here shortly with Carla. At least, that's what I'm trying to convince myself. The mounting uneasiness in my belly is telling me otherwise though.

I have to fight not to leap from my tree and sprint off looking for Liam. He's been too long, and I know something isn't right. How long am I supposed to wait here for? I look around for the others, hoping to gauge their thoughts but they're remarkably well hidden this time.

I swallow hard and quiet my fingers again, schooling myself to stillness. This is what I need to do for now. If I run off after Liam, I will not only give myself away but will most likely cause him to have to come out from hiding before he's ready. It will be a death warrant, not only for me but, most likely, for Liam, Carla, and those left here to fend for themselves.

So, I sit on my uncomfortable perch and do a silent count—one to one hundred, over and over again.

I'm certain Liam has been caught—or worse. I can't hide here any longer. I'm about to start climbing out of the tree when I glimpse black gliding through the trees toward me. Thank all that is good, Liam is okay. I let out a long breath.

The soldier stops and looks up toward me, causing me to catch my breath. It isn't Liam! And after all that waiting I've given us away anyway.

I'm frozen where I am. He looks slowly around the trees, and I hope the others are concealed as well as I thought they were.

"What is it?" A voice calls softly through the trees.

"I thought I heard something," he replies.

A moment later, a second soldier joins him. Together they scan the trees. "It was probably just a squirrel or something," the first soldier says.

"Hey! There's fresh tracks here!" A third soldier calls out.

The first two soldiers frown and, searching the trees again, ready their guns.

One of them whistles and I recognize the command for everyone to gather in.

They're going to gather right under us! All because I was stupid enough to think that any man dressed in black was going to be Liam. Where is he anyway?

The ground is dry with sparse grass and dirt interspersed among prickly bushes. We wouldn't have left any clear tracks, but we ran around below a lot. I wonder if it's possible for them to not realize we've climbed the trees. All it will take is for one person to shift slightly, and we'll be exposed.

I try to relax my grip on my gun. I won't be able to shoot straight if I don't relax. If only we had some way to communicate, we could all take out one soldier each with our first shot. But it just doesn't work when everyone aims at the same person. That was evident last time when the soldier who threatened to shoot me got four bullets in his head, and the other soldiers were left to fire back.

Being careful not to rustle any leaves, I look around for my friends again. There's still no sign of them, which, I suppose, is a good thing.

A little sneeze comes from one of the treetops.

Chapter 23

Dominko crept along the edge of the shadows. He didn't want to go in too deep, afraid of what he might find there— or—what might find him. He knew it was dangerous to be out in the open, but he couldn't convince himself the shadows were his friend. The streets were deathly quiet. He knew from his surveillance there was normally activity in The City at any time of day. The lack of unviables around was making his skin crawl more than the risk of discovery. He forced himself to move deeper into the shadows and concentrated on being even more quiet. He thought he was doing a pretty good job of that.

So far, he hadn't been able to discover where the harvesting might be happening. He knew there was a sizable disused factory just around the next corner. He hadn't gone there directly because he really didn't want to admit the possibility that they would need such a massive space for their nefarious activities. He was still hoping he was wrong about all this; that the two fools at the party had just been blustering. He really hoped he didn't discover anything tonight and that he could go home, call in sick, spend the day in bed, and put this whole conspiracy theory behind him.

He rounded the corner and stopped in the shadows. The building loomed large ahead—and well-lit.

His breathing was coming in loud gasps now. He tried unsuccessfully to quiet it. But freckled cat armpits! Could this really be happening?

He pressed his lips together, squared his shoulders, and started moving forward. He dashed past some stairs, aware that he was out of the shadows as he skirted them. When he got to the other side, he slowed and sought to calm his breathing. He was deeper in the shadows now, less afraid of what they might hold than who might see him from the well-lit building ahead.

"What the crut are you doing here?" A familiar high-pitched voice exclaimed from just behind him.

Dominko jumped in the air and squealed.

A firm grip grabbed his wrist and pulled him deeper into the shadows and pressed him against the wall. "Quiet," another familiar voice growled.

Dominko stifled his whimpers. No one was hurting him. Not yet anyway. He wracked his brain, trying to place the voices. They were so familiar, he felt as if he knew them as well as his best friends—if he had best friends.

"Go see if anyone is following him," the second voice ordered. Dominko didn't hear anyone move to obey. He didn't hear anything. He could have been standing in the dark all alone for all he could hear or see. Only the arm holding him against the wall told him there was someone else there.

Inexplicably, after he got over his initial shock, his fear fled. He actually felt safer now than he had since starting on the night's ill-advised venture.

They waited in silence until a young voice spoke beside him. "It's all clear."

"We need to get him out of here."

"Ollie? Is that you?"

"Of course it's me, you great oaf. If it warn't me, you'd a had your neck sliced by now. Drimmy, you take him back to the door."

"I'm not leavin'. You take him."

"I'm not going back yet. I need to find out what they're doing in that factory," Dominko replied.

Silence greeted him. Dominko pushed Ollie's arm away. The small man wasn't enough to hold him when Dominko wasn't shocked out of his wits. He started heading for the factory again.

"Wait. You can't go there. They've got guards. Come with us. We'll tell you everything you want to know."

Dominko was tempted, but he had to see this for himself. Had to see who was there. He had to see what kind of scale they were operating on. Had to see if it was really happening. "I've come here to see for myself; I don't need any more second-hand information," Dominko said and continued forward.

Ollie sighed.

"I don't trust him, this could be a trap," Drimmy said out of the darkness.

"He's saved us more than once in Hollowcrest. We never could have gotten Sample out of Clone Industries if it warn't for him. Now we're in The City, and I reckon we need to return the favor," Ollie replied.

"Fine, but if he gets seen, I'm not sticken' around to get caught wiv him," Drimmy replied.

"You go check it out. We'll follow," Ollie said to Drimmy. Then to Dominko, "Come on then... I don't suppose you could try to walk quieter."

"I thought I was walking quieter."

Silence was Ollie's only reply.

Dominko made his way forward in the darkness. He kept to the deeper shadows now, heedful of Ollie and Drimmy's warnings and trusting that the kid would warn them if there was anything lurking in them they needed to be wary of. He couldn't hear or see anything. Ollie could be just in front of him or miles away for all Dominko knew.

Dominko kicked another metal container in the dark. It clanked along the old pavement, the sound echoing off the buildings through the still night. "I really am trying," he murmured.

"Ssst!" Ollie's whisper came from way ahead. Dominko started moving faster, but a moment later a hand gripped his wrist. He squealed again.

"Must you keep doing that?" Ollie growled.

"But how did you get there?" Dominko asked.

"Questions later, just be quiet, follow me, and stop kicking things!" Ollie murmured.

Dominko squeezed his lips shut. It was probably a reasonable request. Ollie kept a hold of Dominko's wrist, and Dominko sought to creep quietly behind him.

They came to a stop.

"Do you reckon he can even climb?" Drimmy's small voice queried.

"Of course I can climb," Dominko puffed his chest out. He might not be quiet, but he was strong; there was no call to be questioning that.

"Follow me then," Drimmy's tone suggested he didn't believe Dominko in the least.

The small boy dashed across the street. Dominko held his breath, waiting for a cry of alarm, but the night remained silent. Dominko looked up and down the street. Not a soul stirred, no shadows shifted; there wasn't even a breeze to ruffle the stillness. He felt safer now he was with Ollie and Drimmy, but the building looming over him filled him with dread.

Shadows began to stir around him and three bodies sprinted out into the open and headed for different parts of the factory.

"What the?" Dominko hadn't even realized there was anyone else nearby.

"Sst," whispered Ollie. "Your turn. Follow Drimmy."

Dominko took a deep breath and sprinted in the direction Drimmy had taken. He ran as quickly and as quietly as he could, but he really was beginning to feel like a big oaf. Maybe this was a bad idea. He should have gone back to somewhere safe, if anywhere in The City could be counted as safe, and learned what he could from Ollie. He seemed to know what he was doing.

He reached the relative safety of the shadows on the other side of the street and pushed himself against the wall where he stood, taking in deep lungfuls of air. He hadn't run far; he didn't need a psychiatrist to tell him that his loss of breath was from fear.

"Come on then," Drimmy whined beside him. The boy grabbed his wrist and pulled Dominko after him. Dominko tried to keep up despite tripping over numerous obstacles in the dark. *Are all unviables engineered with enhanced sight or something? Why am I the only one tripping over everything?*

When they reached the side of the building and Dominko saw the scaffolding that Drimmy was already scurrying up, he regretted his inward whining. The problem wasn't the climb. He could climb that, he told himself. It would be easy. Though, he wouldn't do it in as obnoxious a way as Drimmy had—swinging up as if he were a monkey instead of an unviable clone. The real problem was that he could see it.

He would rather feel his way up in the dark than risk being seen.

A yell from the other side of the building was followed by more yells. Dominko looked around in alarm.

"Get a move on," Ollie ordered from beside him. Dominko jumped but preened when he realized he hadn't cried out. He gave Ollie a smug grin, or at least he smiled in the direction Ollie's voice had come from. Whether Ollie could see it or not, Dominko didn't know. For that matter, Dominko had no clue as to whether Ollie was even still there.

They must be creating a diversion on the other side of the building, Dominko realized. Before Ollie could tell him again, Dominko took a deep breath, stepped out of the deep shadows, and began the climb up the rickety scaffolding, hoping it would hold his weight.

Sweat covered Dominko's body by the time he reached Drimmy. The small boy gave him a withering glare but refrained from saying anything. Dominko looked around for Ollie but he was gone.

Drimmy gestured with his chin and Dominko moved forward so he could look through the grimy window in front of him.

"Move to the side, rat brains. You trying to get me killed?" Drimmy's voice was quiet but he still managed to convey plenty of disgust in his tone, and the accompanying shove left no room for doubt. Dominko moved back in confusion. Hadn't Drimmy just gestured for him to look through the window? Drimmy sighed and moved to the side of the window. He leaned against the wall and peered around the edge of the frame so that very little of his head and none of his body would be visible from within if someone chanced to look up.

Dominko waited for him to move out the way and then, carefully, imitated him. He waited for another scathing remark and when none came was hopeful he was doing it right.

It took a moment for his eyes to adjust to the light and manage to see through the grimy window. Movement within resolved into bodies. There were people working inside—too many people. Though the outside of the building was as rundown and filthy as the rest of The City, the inside was pristine. Shiny metal benches gleamed in rows. Fridges lined the walls, and medical equipment was neatly housed in stations around the room.

"They haven't begun yet," he murmured.

"Na, but it won't be long," Drimmy replied. "You seen enough yet?"

Dominko nodded. He could try to pretend it was a hospital being set up, but even *his* denial skills weren't that advanced. There was only one reason anyone would invest that kind of expense in The City, and it wasn't for the good of the unviables. He peeled his eyes away from the window and began the climb back down.

Chapter 24

It's surprising how much stiller you can get than perfectly still. Every one of my muscles stiffens.

The soldiers below haven't frozen. Their guns are already aimed at the leaves that hide Zee.

I fire, hitting one of the soldiers in the head. Other soldiers drop as well, as the trees erupt in a storm of bangs.

Zee falls from her tree, and a soldier levels his gun at her. I shoot at him and watch as his face explodes. One of the soldiers turns his gun toward me. I fire, taking him in the throat.

I feel nauseous, but I keep on firing. The soldiers fall and, despite how well hidden we are, so do Brody and Jake.

When all the soldiers are down, Darla shoots each one again for good measure. I scan through the trees as far as I can see. No more black gives anyone away. Caution tells me to wait and see whose attention we may have attracted, but my friends are injured.

I scurry down my tree and race for Zee. She's been shot in the stomach. There's blood seeping through her clothes where she clutches her belly. I lower my walls and relax as my energy flows to her and the pain begins to leave her face.

"Sample! We need you here!" Dante calls. I'm not finished with Zee, but she's well enough now to wait for me.

With an effort, I pull my walls back up and race to where Dante is crouching over Jake. He's lying on the ground making a horrible gurgling sound. "He's been hit in the lungs, and they're filling with blood. I have to get the bullet out, but he'll drown or bleed out before I can hope to glue him back together, if I even could with these injuries," says Dante.

"So, you get the bullet out. I heal him," I say with a nod.

"Okay," says Dante with a deep breath. He's already armed with a clean, sharp knife and has torn Jake's clothes from his chest. He slips the knife into the wound, ignoring Jake's gurgled attempt at a scream.

I fight to keep my walls up as Dante works. Jake is in so much pain. Fear grips me that any of his gurgled breaths will be his last. It wouldn't be that bad if I healed him with the bullet still in, would it? But Dante has his knife in his chest and there's no way healing him around that could be a good thing.

I hold my breath, willing Dante to work faster.

"Got it," breathes Dante, leaning back with a fist full of bloody metal—knife, and what I presume is a bullet.

I lower my wall, and my energy rushes from me. I fight not to lower it all the way, but my energy is eager to heal, and my emotions are in full support, so it's not easy to keep it under control.

I do my best though. I still need to finish healing Zee, and I don't know how bad Brody is or whether anyone else was injured.

I watch Jake as his breathing starts to come more easily and the fear leaves his face. I wonder what exactly the healing power is doing, but I have no idea what is going on inside his body. All I know is that I'm starting to feel weaker and Jake is starting to look a lot better. At least I seem to be able to do more healing now without collapsing as quickly as I used to, sometimes I feel like my tank is getting bigger and I'm able to hold more energy.

Jake sits up and, with a small smile, nods toward Dante and me, "Thank you, Dante. Thank you, Sample."

"All pain gone?" I ask.

He nods, "I feel great."

I smile back and then head for Brody. "What's wrong with you grump?" I ask.

He scowls at me. "If we were back at the cave, I would decline such a gracious offer of help," he says.

"Sure you would," I reply. "And after such a graceful exit from your tree."

"Are you here to chat or fix me?"

I grin. "Is the bullet out?" I ask.

"It went straight through," he groans.

I lower my walls, and more of my energy rushes out. Despite how sparing I'm trying to be, I can feel my levels getting low. A sharp headache has started up behind my eyes. I lean against a tree to stop from falling over. As the rush of energy leaving my body starts to slow, I realize I have my eyes closed. I open them to see Brody examining the bullet hole in the top of his trousers and all the blood covering him.

"Too bad you can't heal and clean clothes as well. Now that would be something to be proud about," he says.

I try to think of a smart comeback, but my head is sluggish, and I can't concentrate. I do know I need to get back to Zee. I stagger in her direction. My vision is black around the edges making it hard to navigate. I stumble over and through small coarse bushes but eventually make it to collapse at her side.

"You're not giving me more of your energy," she says, but even in my reduced state, I can hear the pain in her voice. I lower my walls again. The last of the light finally fades from my vision.

A sharp pain cuts across my throbbing headache, startling me back to alertness. "Sample! Raise your walls!" Zee commands me, and I realize she just slapped me.

Are my walls down? I check and find she's right. In fact, I'm almost on empty. I fight to raise them and slowly manage to seal them off.

I fall back on the ground and rest my pounding head while fighting the urge to throw up.

"Sample, we need to move out. Take some of my energy," I recognize Connor's voice.

I ignore him. I'm not taking anyone's energy.

"Sample, we need to check on Liam and Carla. He's been gone too long. It worries me that he didn't come when we needed him. That gunfight would have been heard for miles around," says Adam.

Liam! Why isn't he here? I try to sit up, but my body is heavier than lead.

"Please take some of my energy Sample," Connor repeats.

I need to help Liam! I feel a hand take mine. I concentrate on its warmth. I can sense the energy buzzing around in Connor's body and in another one standing beside him. I pull gently, and power rushes into me. I stop and sit up, my eyes going straight to Connor who's sitting beside me. His hand is at his temple, but he smiles at me, "That wasn't too bad," he says.

Adam sways on his feet beside him and steadies himself with a hand on Connor's shoulder. "You took energy from me too," he says.

"Are you okay?" I ask in a high-pitched voice.

"Yeah, I'm fine. It just took me by surprise."

"I didn't mean too," I reply, getting ready to return their energy if they need it.

"It's okay Sample. I feel okay, and it's better if you take energy from a few of us instead of just one person. We can share it around. Just think how much you can do if we all share energy with you," says Adam.

I'm shaking my head. "We still don't know how it will affect you," I say.

Dante recovered fine. It's true; he did seem to make a full recovery even though we have been pushing ourselves hard.

Admittedly, I did give some of his energy back to him, but not all of it.

"We need to get to Liam," I say, rising to my feet. Discussing this won't change anything, but I determine to keep my eyes on Adam and Connor to see how they recover.

"Does anyone else need healing?" I ask Dante.

He shakes his head, "Nothing that will slow them unduly."

"Let's move out!" Adam orders.

I'm already sprinting back in the direction Liam took. I still have a faint headache, and my body is weak. My energy is still below half, and I'm pleased I was able to control how much I took from Adam and Dante, but it means I'm moving slower now than I would like.

I run for a while, leaving the others behind. Trees, small bushes, sparse grass, and dirt surround me in every direction. It doesn't take me long to realize I have no idea of how to find Liam. I slow to a walk and listen, searching the brush for any broken branches and the dirt for boot prints.

There doesn't seem to be anything different about this patch of forest than the last or the next. Birds chirp around me. I try to listen farther afield.

Nothing.

I continue walking, searching the brush, and listening.

Sweat is pouring from me, and my breathing is coming in shallow gasps when a distant whistle reaches my ears.

Stopping and closing my eyes, I listen. A reply whistle gives me an idea of their direction.

My breath comes more easily now that I have a direction to run in. I fly through the trees, slowing only when I near where I thought the whistle was.

Finding a larger trunk, I press my back to it and scan the forest behind me. Nothing moves except the birds in the trees, though there are less of them here than before. This time, I keep my eyes open as I listen. A fat lot of good I'll do Liam if a soldier creeps up on me while I'm trying to rescue him. A part of me is still hoping Liam will creep up on me, but I'm pretty sure that's just wishful thinking.

No more whistles meet my ears, so I peer around my trunk. There's nothing but trees and low scrub to see. I begin creeping through the forest, searching the area, flitting from one trunk to the next, hoping to avoid detection from any scouting soldiers.

Now that I'm here, I realize how foolish it was to leave the others behind. There's a much higher chance that a soldier will discover me than the other way around, and it's a certainty they'd beat me in a fight.

Liam needs me though, so I firm my resolve and continue my search.

I'm hiding behind a tree and trying to see through some thick brush when the hairs on my neck start standing on end. I have a terrible feeling I'm being watched. I pull my head back and search the forest behind me. I still can't see anyone, but all the birds have gone quiet.

Chapter 25

Men's voices reach me. I take a deep, quiet breath and, ignoring my fear, creep through the forest toward them.

The voices aren't loud, but there does seem to be an argument happening. The bushes are a lot thicker in this area, allowing me places to hide as I draw near to the soldiers.

Their voices become clearer until I reach a thick copse of prickly brush and peer through to see the soldiers. Without disturbing the leaves at all, I crouch down between a couple of bushes that completely hide me on two sides.

By moving my head around, I'm able to peer through the thick brush to see the soldier's camp. There are eight of them there. More than I expected, given how many we already killed. Unless this is a different crew. If that's the case, there are probably more from this crew out scouting. I glance back over my shoulder.

Biting my lip, I turn back to the soldier's camp. I need to find Liam and Carla.

Four soldiers are standing in heated conversation. There are some neatly packed backpacks stacked together with attached bedrolls. A campfire has been doused. Two men are on watch; though fortunately, are not looking this way at the moment. Another two are working on something on the ground on the other side of the camp.

They're speaking, but it's hard to hear what they're saying over the closer soldier's conversation. One of them strikes forward with a knife. A flash of blonde hair and a spray of blood reveals Carla struggling against them.

"No!" Liam's roar draws my attention to the tree where he's bound. He's been stripped of his jacket and shirt and is just in his trousers and a black singlet. His muscles bulge as he struggles in a mad fury, and then he's leaping away from the tree with a rope hanging from his wrists. He charges the men around Carla.

A gunshot explodes through the air making me jump. Red spreads across Liam's chest, and his eyes go wide before he collapses to the ground.

No! My feet are moving before I have time to think. I jump from behind my bush and sprint across the camp toward him.

"Stop where you are!"

"Stop or I'll shoot!" Soldiers are yelling, but all I know is that Liam is dying or already dead.

I skid on my knees to stop beside him.

There's blood everywhere. His eyes are closed and there's more blood bubbling from his mouth as he labors to breathe.

I lower my walls, and my energy flows toward him. It won't be enough! Now I wish I took more from Connor and Adam. I keep feeding him energy, but blood is spurting from him, and my reserves are getting dangerously low.

I can't let Liam die! A soldier reaches out to grab me. I turn and seize his wrist. He pulls his other hand back to punch me, but before he can, I suck his energy. I need it for Liam, and I don't hesitate to take all I can. Any resistance I previously felt about taking people's energy is gone. I will heal Liam.

The soldier collapses.

I hear guns cocked around me. I don't hesitate. If they stop me, then Liam dies. I suck the energy out of all of them. They fall to the ground, and health and vitality fill me. I feel more alive than I've ever felt. I push the energy toward Liam.

He jolts upright with a loud gasp.

Laughing aloud, I stand and twirl in circles, my arms flung wide.

Liam leaps to his feet and sprints to Carla's side. A wave of guilt rushes over me, and I run to join them.

She's gasping and clutching her stomach. I release energy to her, and the pain leaves her face. She leans back with a contented expression.

"Wow, that feels good," she sighs.

"I know!" I exclaim. "I've got so much energy I don't know what to do with it all. I feel like I could fly!" I'm giddy with all the power rushing through me.

My gaze goes to Liam. He's checking the pulse of one of the soldiers. My exuberance flees.

"I didn't kill them, did I?"

"No," he shakes his head, and I breathe out in relief.

Liam reaches down beside the soldier and picks up his gun. He stands and shoots the soldier in the head.

"No!" I yell, rushing toward him as he stalks toward the next soldier, his face a grim mask.

Carla tackles me, holding me back. I kick at her, trying to fight free. The gun explodes again, and tears stream down my cheeks.

"No! What are you doing?" I scream.

"Sample, he has to," Carla pleads with me.

"No," I gasp as the gun sounds again.

I shove Carla away, managing to break free and run for Liam.

Launching myself at him, I careen into his legs. It's like hitting a boulder. I clutch at his arm, pulling myself up, begging him to stop. He turns pain filled eyes on me; but then his expression turns hard again. He turns his back on me and all his muscles tense. I yank at his arm, but it doesn't budge. He shoots again.

I can't stop him. I'm not strong enough. He strides toward the next soldier, but I run in front of him and lay over the soldier's chest, shielding him from Liam. Sobs wrack my body. "Stop, please stop."

"Sample, I have to."

Another shot explodes. I jump, looking around for the threat. Carla has shot one of the downed soldiers. Face grim, she runs for the next soldier and shoots him in the head as well.

"You're animals!" I scream.

I grab a gun from the soldier beside me and aim it at Liam. "Stop now or I shoot!" I yell.

Liam's shoulders fall, but Carla snorts in disbelief. She takes aim and shoots again. There's only one soldier left. The one I'm protecting.

I shake my head at Liam. "Don't make me do it."

"Sample," he begs.

"How could you? We could have left them. They were no threat to us."

"But they were Sample."

A shot explodes behind me, and I leap up in shock. I swing around to find Carla has come around behind me and shot the last soldier.

"We need to get back and check on the others. All the soldiers are heading back to a location near here today," says Liam as he pulls on his shirt.

Carla is already striding away.

I watch in shock. Is that it? Kill all these people in cold blood and then leave? I look at Liam, trying to find some humanity in him. His face is as hard as steel. My lip curls. Who is this man?

"We don't have time for this now Sample. Are you going to walk, or will I carry you?" I jump away from him and stalk after Carla. I don't want that monster anywhere near me.

We run back through the trees the way I came. None of us talk. I take the lead once we get back to where Liam left us and guide Carla and Liam to the trees where we hid.

The others are gone.

Liam searches for tracks, but the ground has been trampled by the battle we had with the soldiers. His jaw is set in a hard line, and I can't tell what he's thinking. His expression has barely flickered since he started shooting the soldiers. I'm loathe to break the stony silence that surrounds the three of us, but I'm worried about the others wandering around when there are more soldiers coming.

I walk back in the direction I took to find Liam. "They left this way," I say. Liam doesn't even look at me, but he follows my direction and searches the area I indicate.

He doesn't say anything, but when he starts walking off through the trees, Carla and I follow.

We walk for about half an hour, Liam searching the ground and scrub and leading the way.

The too familiar sound of guns firing reaches us.

We break into a sprint and race toward the sound. It's not our friends we find, however, but soldiers—soldiers firing into the treetops.

"Not again! How many are there in this forest?"

The three of us jump behind trees and open fire on the soldiers. I'm using real bullets, as are Liam and Carla. I realize with a start that Liam swapped out all his paralyzing bullets for real ones when we first started facing the soldiers. He's been shooting to kill the whole time. Does he hate his own kind that much? He's never shot to kill before, unless it was for food.

More soldiers pour into the clearing from the other side and start firing at the treetops. With that many soldiers shooting, it will be impossible to miss my friends even if they can't see who they're shooting at.

I know I can stop this immediately. All I need to do is suck the energy out of the soldiers, but the picture of Liam and Carla shooting unconscious people in the head is too vivid. I can't be party to that again.

Chapter 26

The trek through The City to Ollie and Drimmy's hideout was an adventure in itself. Though Dominko breathed easier once he was out of sight of the factory, he knew there were still many dangers lurking in the shadows. Between Ollie, Drimmy, and the woman who had joined them on their way back, they managed to avoid any threats. Still, weaving through back alleys, up and down stairways, and across rooftops was an experience Dominko had never had before. He was glad he kept fit, or he wouldn't have been able to keep up. Leaping from one roof to another sent Dominko's heart racing every time, but when they finally stopped, by a metal trapdoor on a rooftop, he could feel his mouth stretched in a wide grin. He felt alive like he hadn't in a long time.

Dominko followed the others down the stairs. They were still moving quietly, so he did his best to imitate them, even though he was bursting with questions.

They ghosted along a dimly lit corridor and opened one of the many doors that lined it. He followed them inside and stood in the dark wondering where to go. The woman pushed him farther in, so she could enter, and he heard the door close softly behind her. A light switched on ahead of

Dominko, revealing a cleaner's closet. Old buckets, brooms, and plastic containers littered the dust and cobweb filled floor and shelves. Beyond the small room Dominko shared with the woman was another room that looked exactly the same, and beyond that, another.

Dominko began to weave his way forward, following the trail of dust-free floor where countless feet had worn it clean. He could see Ollie's white head of hair ahead. It was moving away, so Dominko quickened his pace to catch up. He'd just entered the third room when a shadow moved beside him. Dominko squealed and leaped into the air.

A snigger sounded beside him, and Dominko looked down to see a skinny, sore pocked man lounging in a corner.

Dominko scowled at the man. There was no call to be sniggering. It was impolite to scare people like that, and he was sure if their positions were reversed, the man would have let out a manly yelp of surprise just like Dominko had.

He rushed after Ollie, keeping a careful eye out for others hiding in dirty corners. It was only two more small rooms before Dominko caught up with Ollie and Drimmy, who had stopped in a slightly bigger room, and found metal drums to perch on.

Dominko looked around at what could only be described as a large closet. Others were crowding in around him. Is this where they had been bringing him? What for? "I thought we were going back to your base?" Dominko said.

Drimmy curled his nose up, and Dominko turned toward Ollie, hoping for a less scathing explanation.

"This is our base," was Ollie's short reply.

Dominko looked around. It was hard to see anything past all the bodies that were in the room and the two rooms on either side, but on a high shelf in the next room, he glimpsed a body lying under a threadbare gray blanket. With a sinking feeling in his stomach, it dawned on him that this wasn't just their base of operations, but probably where they lived as well.

"Who's this?" a woman asked.

"This is Dominko," Ollie replied.

"Is he going to stay here?" a woman cackled. A roar of laughter met her question. Dominko frowned at those around him. He didn't see what was so funny.

"He came to The City to investigate the new harvesting base. We brought him back here to fill him in."

"Why?" A man asked.

"Dominko saved ours and Sample's lives more than once when we were in Hollowcrest."

"I thought you said you was staying with the Jesus lover?" A voice accused. "He don't look like he loves nobody but himself."

Drimmy sniggered, and Dominko turned a hurt look upon him. "What?" Drimmy asked with his hands out to the side and an impish grin.

"There's not much new to report," Ollie said, turning the conversation away from Dominko. "They've pretty much completed setting up at their new location and will probably begin using it soon."

"Why do you keep saying new?" Dominko asked.

"This is the second factory we know of," Ollie replied. They've been operating out of a smaller one for some time now. That's what brought us back to The City."

"How did you get back here?" Dominko asked.

"Ahem," someone cleared their throat. "We need to start planning."

Ollie waved them away. "You've already started planning; there's nothing new to add right now. Continue brainstorming. We'll talk in the morning. I need some time to digest what I saw tonight.

"What did you see?" A woman asked.

Ollie shrugged. "Nothing new. But … it's so big. And there's so many workers. Too many workstations. It's terrifying."

Dominko swallowed against a lump in his throat. He'd thought it was horrifying, but for these people it was different. It could be them or their friends on those tables next week or next month, or the month after that, and who was to tell if it would ever stop.

"Go," Ollie said again, waving everyone away. "We will strategize in the morning."

"Strategize for what?" Dominko asked.

Ollie gave him a long searching look, causing Dominko to squirm under his piercing gaze.

Slowly people shuffled out of the room. When there was room to move, Ollie gestured at a drum. "Have a seat."

Drimmy sniggered. "Yeah right. His royal highness wouldn't want to get his precious clothes dirty."

Dominko looked down at his outfit. He was wearing gym clothes! He looked at the drum. It did look like it could harbor countless germs. He refused to be mocked further by Drimmy though, so he moved toward the drum and awkwardly jumped up to land his backside on it.

A well-rounded, blonde sex clone walked into the room and leaned against Ollie's arm. Dominko stretched out his neck muscles, trying to exercise some patience. He had had enough of beautiful women monopolizing his time in Hollowcrest. He was hoping to escape them here. He waited for an inane comment to come out of her mouth. Before she spoke, she turned the most amazing blue eyes Dominko had ever seen, on him. Dominko gasped, then shook his head clear. There was only so long a pair of eyes could keep him interested. Until he could find a woman of substance, he couldn't be bothered wasting time on their vanity.

He decided to pretend she wasn't there and ask Ollie what he knew about the harvesting, but one look at Ollie's face was enough to cause a bark of laughter to erupt from him.

Ollie looked like he was constipated, his face dark red and his eyes staring at nothing in the opposite direction of the woman.

"What's so funny?" the woman asked.

Dominko tried to talk through his laughter. "You," he gestured, "He …" Dominko couldn't finish his sentence.

The woman looked at Ollie and, seeing his discomfort, took a step back. "Oh, I'm sorry. I really have been working on it."

Despite himself, Dominko's curiosity got the better of him. "Working on what?"

219

"On not being so alluring."

Dominko erupted in a fresh round of laughter. Finally, he managed to speak. "They're words I never expected to hear from a woman."

She merely shrugged and turned her attention back to Ollie who was still staring at the wall.

"Ollie, what was the medical equipment like?"

He gestured wildly in Drimmy's direction. "Ask the boy, he saw it."

She turned to Drimmy with raised eyebrows.

"Bianka, why do you keep wasting our time with these questions? I've told you before, they're shiny and sharp. It don't matter what they look like, it's what they're gonna do wiv 'em that matters."

"I know," she sighed, "It's just that so much good could be done, you know. There's a man downstairs with this huge growth on his face. He can hardly speak anymore, and it's heading for his eye. I think I could cut it out, you know. If I had something clean and sharp enough, and painkillers..." Drimmy rolled his eyes and turned away from her. She continued listing the things she would need, seemingly having forgotten that anyone else was in the room. Dominko was about to add his own speculation about how best to go about the operation when Ollie interrupted him.

"What are you doing here Dominko?"

"I could ask you the same question. I thought you were safely sequestered at Finn's."

"We couldn't stay there. Not when we heard what was happening."

"But how did you hear? And how did you get through the wall?"

"Finn has his sources. You'd be shocked by how much that man knows."

"But he hasn't spoken up."

"Not yet. He doesn't have any evidence yet. That's part of why we're here; to get evidence. Unfortunately, while it's completely obvious what's going on to those with eyes to see, we haven't got any tangible proof of what they're doing."

"But how'd you get here?"

Ollie gestured at Drimmy. "The kid spent weeks of nights scouting the wall until he found the door they were leaving unlocked."

"You could have just come to me," Dominko said.

"Really?" Ollie's tone was dry. "Leaving aside the fact that you've been noticeably absent since Sample left, just say we had of come to you with the information we had, you would have believed us? And even if you had, would you have been on our side? You're pretty tight in your father's pocket."

Dominko's jaw dropped open. "I am not," his voice had risen an octave in, what he believed to be, righteous indignation. He wanted to think he would have believed them. They were his friends. "I had to keep my distance, to keep you both safe. My father has my every move watched, if I had visited Finn, he would have found you for sure."

"The house is surrounded by soldiers doing surveillance. You already know they know we're there. You're the one who uploaded our cover stories into the system."

Dominko shook his head. "That's just routine surveillance. They know they can't kill Finn now, but they're still keeping an eye on him. If I were to visit, it would draw my father's attention, and you don't want that."

"Whatever," said Drimmy. "What are you doing here?"

"I heard rumors, and there were things just not adding up, or adding up too well in the wrong way. I had to investigate."

"So what are you gonna do about it now you've investigated it?" asked Drimmy.

Dominko's eyes expanded. He hadn't considered doing anything. What could he do?

"Me? Well, you know I'd like to do something, but I don't have any influence or power. Maybe, I could tell my father, and he can put a stop to it," even as he said the words he knew that would be a terrible mistake.

"You've got to be kidding," said Drimmy.

"Or the law enforcers. It's their job to maintain the law."

"'Cause that worked out so well last time," responded Ollie.

"Well, what are you going to do?"

Ollie sighed. "Drimmy will take word back to Finn, and I'll stay here to organize disruptions."

"Disruptions?"

"Guerrilla warfare!" Bianka answered with delight. Dominko glanced at her in surprise, and Ollie chuckled.

"Well, that might be exaggerating what we have planned. We can't do so much they need to bring soldiers in, but we can make things disappear and interrupt their travels between the factory and the Wall," said Ollie.

"They can't send the soldiers in; they belong to my father."

No one replied, but Dominko didn't like the tone of Ollie's long stare.

Dominko squirmed. "Even without the soldiers, your people will get hurt."

"People are gonna get hurt anyway," Ollie mumbled.

"They'll be locking the door again soon," said Drimmy.

"Alright. Off with you then. Be safe. Take Dominko with you," ordered Ollie.

"But, he's so slow and loud," whined Drimmy.

"Would you rather I keep him here?"

Dominko looked around in alarm, and Drimmy giggled.

"I'll be fast, I promise. Fast and quiet," Dominko pleaded.

"Come on then," Drimmy replied, still chuckling.

As Dominko followed him to the adjoining room, he heard Bianka ask Ollie a question, "If you're going to be stealing the medical equipment, can you bring it back to me?"

Pushing the woman from his mind, he raced after the boy who was already leaving him behind.

Chapter 27

A scream pierces the air. Tears stream down my cheeks. My friends will all die. It's them or the soldiers. It's up to me.

A roar of anger tears from my throat as I begin to pull the soldier's energy out of them. There are so many soldiers and too much power, but I keep on pulling. I yell in fury at all the killing, fury at Liam for forcing me to make this choice. I don't want to kill anyone, but I suck the soldier's life force from them until they all collapse to the ground.

I stalk into the clearing the soldiers are lying in. I don't bother checking if they're still alive. Liam will probably just kill them now that I've made it easy for him. I don't spare a glance for him or Carla.

I can't see my friends. None of them have climbed down yet. I don't even know if any of them still live. My whole body is tingling and feels like it's expanded with energy. I lower my walls a little and force the energy upward, careful not to let any of it near the soldiers on the ground.

Gasps sound from the treetops.

"Crut Sample. I hadn't removed the bullet yet," Dante says.

I shrug. I can't seem to find it in me to care.

"Ow! Ow! Ow!" Ethan says as he climbs out of the same tree as Dante.

The others follow slowly. I frown at Ethan and send more energy toward him. It doesn't seem to alleviate the twist of pain on his face.

Dante reaches his side and after a quick examination turns to me and says, "Sample, we really need to get the bullets out before you heal people."

"We need to move," Liam says. "All the soldiers will be converging near here this afternoon. If we don't get out of here fast, we won't escape."

"Aren't you going to murder everyone first?" I ask. "Or have you got that out of your system now?"

I look around at the soldiers. Their necks are cut. "You didn't?" I accuse Liam, my voice barely audible.

He barely shakes his head. I look around to see Jake slicing the neck of a soldier. I stare at him in horror.

"What is wrong with you people?" I ask.

"We need to remove the bullets from everyone," says Dante.

"There's no time. You can do it later," Liam replies.

"Ethan can't travel like this," Dante argues.

"Fine," Liam sighs. "Fix him, but then we leave." He gestures me forward.

I glare at him. Does he really think he can tell me what to do?

"Sample, I need you," says Dante.

With one last stink eye for Liam to make sure he doesn't think I'm doing it because he told me to, I walk to Dante and Ethan.

Liam joins us, and I'm about to tell him to leave when he hands Ethan a thick stick to put in his mouth and then pins his shoulders to the ground.

Dante grits his teeth and pushes his knife into Ethan's hip. Ethan grunts, his whole body convulsing against the pain. I lean all my weight on Ethan's legs to hold him still while Dante digs deeper, looking for the bullet.

This is my fault. I let all that power go to my head. I didn't think about what I was doing at all. This is so much worse for Ethan than if Dante had gotten the bullet out before I healed him. I look around at the others who are collecting weapons and ammunition from the soldiers and wonder how many of them have got bullets buried in them because of me.

"Got it," says Dante, drawing my attention back to Ethan. With a sigh of relief, I leak some energy to him. He stops straining against me, and I move off his legs. The flesh in his new wound seals together, followed by layers of skin.

Liam releases his shoulders and Ethan pulls the stick from his mouth. He jumps to his feet and does a couple of stretches. "Well I can move now, but I'm not sure it was worth it," he says with a smile for us.

I grab my pack and Jake hands me some ammunition. I take it without meeting his eyes. I feel dirty just being near him.

"Ready?" Adam asks us. Dante nods. Adam gestures for Liam to take the lead. He pauses, listening.

I breathe deeply, trying to find a measure of calm. I don't want to be with these people anymore. Liam lopes into the forest, and the others fall in quietly behind him. As I take up the rear, I consider branching off on my own. The forest is going to be full of soldiers, but I can probably slip by them unnoticed if I'm on my own, and if any do find me, I can always render them unconscious. At least that way, I won't be contributing to their murder.

But what will happen when I reach Hollowcrest. I can always find Finn and the family, but none of them are trained for warfare. Even with this crew, our chances of any form of success are limited, but we'll have a better chance than if I try to do it on my own.

Bile fills my mouth as I realize this bloodthirsty group might be my best chance of saving the unviables in The City.

Dante falls back to jog beside me.

"That was pretty awful what Jake did," he says.

Some of the tension leaves my body. Someone feels the same as me.

"It was necessary though," he says.

I turn a dark look on him. "They were unconscious. We could have been away before they even woke," I reply.

He nods. "Of course. But what do you think they would do once they woke?"

I shrug. "Even if they did follow us, I could have taken their energy from them again."

"That would have been the best-case scenario. But what if you couldn't do it again? You are still new at this."

I start to reply, but he cuts me off. "I doubt they would have all followed us though. Your power is something completely outside their experience. Most likely, they would have sent at least one person back to report."

I shrug. I don't want to lend credence to what he's saying.

"If their superiors get word of what you can do, we won't be facing isolated groups. They will send everyone they've got out here after us, and from what Liam said about their training exercises, that's thousands. As much as I hate what Jake did, we couldn't escape if thousands came after us."

I feel ill. I can't admit that what Liam, Carla, and Jake did was right.

"Jake probably saved our lives," Dante continues. "I know Jake though. He's not an engineered soldier without a conscience." His words pierce me, but I'm not thinking about Jake. Liam hates that he's a soldier, engineered to kill. He hates killing, that's why he's always used paralyzing bullets; risked his life numerous times because he didn't want to kill people outright when he could. To kill so ruthlessly, as he did, would be undermining everything he's tried to be, everything he's tried not to be.

"What Jake did will be eating him up inside, he would do anything to protect us and the innocents we're going to try and help, but it was at a terrible cost to himself."

I look forward to where Liam leads the group. His back is rigid even as he moves through the trees with a silent grace.

"Hopefully, we can be there enough for him to show him he is a good person," Dante finishes.

He glances at me, but I'm feeling too much to know how to respond.

Can I get past my own feelings of revulsion enough to show Liam I still believe he's good? Do I still believe he is good? What he did might have been necessary, but it was still wrong.

"It was a great act of sacrifice on Jake's part. I couldn't do what he did. He saved our lives," says Dante.

I lower my head slightly in acknowledgment.

I'm glad when Dante pulls ahead of me. He's left me with a lot to ponder.

We move through the trees as quickly and silently as city raised clones can. Liam leads us around groups of soldiers. They're traveling too, and have finished hunting. They're also expecting there to be other groups of soldiers around, so signs of our passing and small noises don't cause them to start tracking us. If anything, it's easier for us to avoid them now. As long as none of them catch a glimpse of us, we should be right. I'm shocked by how many of them there are though. Dante's right, we wouldn't be able to fight them all.

Chapter 28

A peculiar bird noise is the first warning we've been seen. I scan the area but can't see anything. Liam has sidled up to a tree, however, and is holding his gun ready. I find my own trunk and try to calm my erratic breathing.

The others have all found their own trees. We're as ready as we can be, but I still have no idea where the enemy is.

We wait. Every muscle in my body is tense. I listen but can't hear anything other than Noah's fidgeting nearby.

Something moves through the trees, drawing my attention. There's more moving near it. Too quickly, a wall of black-clad bodies reveals itself running toward us, broken only by the trees it washes around. Craning my neck, I look around the other side of my tree. We're surrounded. There's too many of them! How did they organize such a massive attack?

The others open fire, but we can't hope to defeat so many. Some of the soldiers fall to the ground, but there are many more running toward us. They raise their guns. We can't fight our way out of this.

I lower my walls and suck energy for all I'm worth. There are so many people, I don't know how I can possibly contain all the life force, but I keep pulling. Soldiers fall before me, but there are more coming. I draw their energy in as well. I think I'll burst, but I don't. I can't even feel my walls anymore, just life and energy. I feel powerful. A deep longing overwhelms me to heal people, but I can't. Instead, I keep sucking.

The forest is quiet around me. Soldiers litter the ground amongst the trees. Turning to my friends, I see them on the ground as well.

"No!" Noah is the closest to me, and I run to him. Was I too late? I don't think the soldiers started shooting. My friends can't be dead. I reach Noah's side and search him for blood but can't find any. Checking his neck, I find a pulse. I frown. What's wrong with him? I feed him some energy, and he recovers.

"Woah," he says. "Did you get them all?" his voice is groggy.

"Yeah, I think so. What happened to you?"

He smiles. "You happened to me."

I glance around at the others as comprehension dawns on me.

A fresh wave of fear grips me. What if I killed them? I can't heal them all at once in case I heal the soldiers as well. I run to Darla and without waiting to check her pulse, feed her some energy. She recovers, and I run to Jake.

By the time I reach Liam, I'm breathing more easily. Everyone else has recovered. Surely he will as well; still, my heart is hammering in my chest.

I push my energy at Liam. He bolts upright, looking around at our fallen enemy. He nods in my direction but doesn't make eye contact.

"Thank you Sample," he says as he stands.

The others have joined us, and we stand, staring at all the bodies through the trees. With a hard-set jaw, Jake pulls out his knife.

"Leave them," says Liam. "There's no point anymore. They obviously know there's someone other than the usual bush brigands out here. Our best bet is to run and hope they don't get Sample before she can drop them."

With a look of relief, Jake sheathes his knife.

Following Liam, we set off at a run.

The next few days are spent running through the forest, trying to escape soldiers. They're hunting for us now, and even though I'm full of energy and feel more alive than I ever have before, the rest of our group isn't faring as well. I keep trying to feed them extra to sustain them, but they don't seem built to contain it, and it runs out fast with the way we are pushing ourselves and the constant fear that someone will get shot before I can drain every soldier that comes upon us.

I feed some more energy to Connor who's falling behind the others. I'm bringing up the rear so I can make sure everyone's okay. I can't just throw indefinite amounts at them constantly. It takes a lot of concentration to make sure the energy only goes where it's supposed to and not to the enemy. I'm getting better at it though. Better at who I drain it from too. I've learned how to isolate the people whose energy I don't want and how to wall them off, and also to control how much energy I take and how quickly I take it.

I can't help wondering how far the soldiers will follow us though. What will happen if they follow us all the way back to Hollowcrest? I'm not exactly sure what to do when I reach Hollowcrest but arriving with a thousand soldiers on my tail is really not what I had planned.

Biting my lip, I try not to think about what I might have to do. I think I have the power to kill the soldiers following us, and I know they'll kill us if they get the chance, but I don't know if I can convince myself to do it. Dante was right when he said Jake did us all a favor. I don't think I have the strength to execute people like that.

I never wanted to even learn how to use a gun, but I did for self-defense, but this somehow feels different. Maybe it's because the enemy won't have a chance to defend themselves. I will have all the power.

As the landscape becomes more familiar, my anxiety increases. Last time I ran through these foothills, it was with Liam by my side and the hope of finding the Resistance to help with my cause, and, truthfully, a small hope that Liam might one day be mine. I know Liam a lot better now, know his inner strengths and vulnerabilities. Even with his faults, I can't help but love him; but we're further from being together than we ever have been. And now, instead of looking for an army to help us, we're fleeing one. One that I'm pretty sure I can defeat, but also sure that I'll never survive the guilt if I do.

The forest that was never thick is even thinner now, and we often have to sprint from one copse of trees to the next across clear patches. I remember the drive away from Hollowcrest and the seemingly endless open plains. If we don't lose the soldiers before then, I will be left with no choice but to kill them. Unfortunately, with their rejuvenation capacities, they recover too quickly when I just render them unconscious.

I work my way through a thick copse of trees and stop at the edge. A lump forms in my throat. I can see three more trees, and that's it. I'm out of time.

"We'll camp here," says Adam. It's early to stop, but the others are exhausted. They've had barely any sleep in days and are barely standing. I release energy to them, and they brighten a bit, but I know it won't last long. Their bodies are just not made to operate on such little sleep, especially with the constant running, fighting, and fear.

Everything within me is screaming that we need to keep going, but there's no point. We could push the others to the point of collapse, but we will still be clearly visible out in the open. If we haven't lost the soldiers by now, then we're not going to.

I take the first watch. Liam has offered to take the second half of the night, but I won't wake him. I'm so full of energy, sleep is harder to find than it ever has been.

I sit in a tree, peering into the darkness, wishing for the soldier's enhanced eyesight. The night is black, and I know the soldiers can be upon us without making a sound.

Closing my eyes, I revert to my new sense and feel for the lives around me. I can feel the energy from my friends below me; their unique energy signatures that have become so familiar to me. Ignoring them, I seek wider. I don't notice anything, so I feel in an ever-increasing circumference. I'm not sure how far I would be able to sense the approaching soldiers, but I keep trying until I notice Liam approaching my tree.

"My watch. You get some rest," he says. I sigh. He has that tone that suggests I'm not getting out of this without a fight. I climb out of the tree and, pulling my blanket free of my pack, curl up on the cold ground.

I wonder if I'll get to sleep in a bed in Hollowcrest. I mean, I know we're going to be busy, but surely there might be an opportunity for a bed at some point. And a lounge, it's amazing how attached I became to lounges while staying at Finn's and Father Bayle's. And surely I'll be able to use a flushing toilet and toilet paper. A sigh of contentment escapes me at the prospect. The thoughts don't help me to drift off to sleep though. I spend the rest of the night searching for any sense of the approaching soldiers that never come.

Chapter 29

Dominko tried to lounge in the straight-backed chair, but it was impossible. He settled for drumming his fingers on his father's table instead. The twitch in his father's eye wasn't enough to bring a smile to Dominko's face, however. His father continued to lecture his employees who sat around the table receiving their instructions for the week's business transactions and takeover bids. At least, Dominko presumed that was what he was droning on about. Dominko had been even less attentive than usual, if that was possible.

Dominko had intentionally arrived late, wishing to escape his father's lecture about leaving his date early the previous evening. In all probability, he'd merely increased his father's ire, but Dominko was counting on his father not having another chance to lecture him throughout the day as he dealt with his scheduled meetings. The plan was to skip out early with a hurried excuse that he needed to make things up to Francesca before he could receive the coming reprimands.

Carlos shot Dominko another glare. *What have I done now?* Carlos's eyes flicked to Dominko's fingers, and he realized he was still tapping. He stopped, with every intention of starting again in a few minutes. His thoughts drifted back to the night before and what he'd discovered in The City. Against his will, his eyes returned to his father. He couldn't help his growing suspicions about the man. He had thought it impossible that he could have anything to do with harvesting the clone's organs, but he now found himself wondering how something this big could happen under his father's nose without him knowing about it. Would anyone dare? This wasn't some small crime element in an unused basement. This was a major endeavor, and happening right in his father's city.

Security has always been my job. Daddy dearest has never taken an interest in such plebeian work. Dominko tried to convince himself. As much as he detested his father, he didn't want to believe he could be the son of someone who would act so despicably. His father's mind, however, was just as brilliant as Dominko's, but where Dominko loved technology and the mechanics of the human body, Carlos was a political mastermind. He was always two steps ahead of everyone else, and Dominko was finding it hard to believe his father wasn't aware of what was happening—what was being done.

"Dominko!" His father's voice cut into Dominko's thoughts. He looked around the room and realized it was empty.

"Oh crap."

"What is going on with you? You haven't been paying attention at all today and after your behavior last night ..."

What behavior last night? Surely he hadn't been caught by surveillance. Dominko racked his mind to think of any camera he may have missed.

"Francesca's mother rang me this morning with grave concerns about your upcoming marriage."

Dominko expelled a loud breath he hadn't realized he was holding. He waved his hand. "I'll make it up to her tonight."

"Dominko, you are not taking this alliance seriously. You show no interest in learning how to run this business. I'm beginning to think I may need to find myself another heir."

Dominko heard the words as if through a long tunnel. He knew he should take them seriously, but he couldn't seem to focus on them.

"Why did you shut my project down?"

His father stopped his threats, and a look of confusion flashed across his face. "Project? What project?"

"What project?" Dominko spluttered. "My healing clone project!"

"Why are you still talking about that? I did what needed to be done. Don't tell me that is why you've been misbehaving. I don't have time for these juvenile temper tantrums."

No, you never did have time for juveniles. Dominko didn't bother voicing the cutting remark. It wasn't important anymore.

"I was working on a clone that would be able to heal people, that would have made the world a better place. I'd made serious headway. The new samples would have survived. Why..."

"You were working on something that would have killed people!"

Dominko's jaw dropped. His father had stopped doing genetic engineering in the last couple of decades, but Dominko knew he had once been the most brilliant geneticist out there. His father couldn't be this dense.

"What are you talking about?" Dominko asked. "I was working on healing clones! I'm not interested in the soldier clones. Do you think I'd lie to you about it?"

"It wouldn't surprise me at all what you would lie to me about, Dominko. But in this case, I believe it is more an issue of stupidity."

Dominko gaped at him. For all his insults, his father had never accused him of being stupid before.

His father sighed and looked away. "Dominko, there is nothing I want more than to find a way to heal people. If I could have done that sooner, then I never would have lost your …" He stopped and, firming his jaw, looked Dominko in the eye. "I can't believe you didn't see it, Dominko. The very genes you were manipulating to enable those clones to pour energy into people, were the ones that would destroy us."

"None of what you're saying makes sense," Dominko replied.

"The x59 gene also has the capacity to suck energy from people!" Carlos shouted. "I can't believe I'm having this argument again. I thought I was done with that when Falisco—"

"You shut Falisco's project down?" Dominko whispered.

"Well of course I did. He was my head geneticist. Who else could have shut him down?"

"But they were all killed—"

"Not all," his father replied.

"All but one."

Carlos turned sharply to face Dominko. "What do you know about who survived?"

Dominko almost told his father about his visit to The City and Samuel. He was sick of hiding from his father, sick of cowering away, but he remembered in time that it was Samuel's life that was threatened. "I was able to trace everyone's deaths but one," Dominko replied. "Your old best friend."

His father's eyes clouded over for a moment in something that could have been regret. But then they cleared, and their usual sharpness returned. "Why were you researching them?"

"I was looking for information on the project. Most of Falisco's notes were missing. I was hoping to talk about the research with someone."

"Were missing?"

"Are missing," Dominko hastened to reply.

"How did you know how to advance with the research?"

"I figured it out," Dominko puffed out his chest. His father's eyes narrowed in suspicion. Dominko added a smug smile to his charade.

"The healing clones were designed for compassion. They would never seek to harm people," Dominko tried to convince his father.

"Enough!" Carlos roared. Dominko leaned back from the uncharacteristic display of emotion.

"I had enough of these arguments from Falisco and his team. They refused to be silenced. They even threatened to take their research elsewhere. I will have obedience from you Dominko. You will not talk about your research to anyone. I can find another heir easily enough, but I can't find another son."

Dominko was shocked into stillness. *Did daddy dearest just threaten to kill me?*

His father left the room, but it was some time before Dominko found himself ready to follow.

Chapter 30

We run through the streets of Hollowcrest. Despite the imminent chance of discovery, I feel more relaxed than I have in months. It's not The City, but Hollowcrest almost feels like home. I breathe in the scent of concrete and metal as the cold night air brushes past my face. Now that we're out of the wild with its random twigs and dry leaves, the others move almost as quietly as Liam and me.

A car drives past up ahead, and we all move deeper into the shadows of our back alley, pressing our backs to a wall. We have our guns ready but are agreed that my draining of people's energy is a much quieter way to move through Hollowcrest. It worked well enough with the gate guards. They didn't even see us coming; by the time someone discovers our entry on the camera footage, we'll be deep within Hollowcrest.

I follow Liam as he peels away from the wall and continues leading us up the alley. I'm glad I didn't have to try to find my way to Finn's on my own. I have no idea where we are or what direction we're going in.

Butterflies stir in my stomach. They have to be there, have to be alright.

We sprint across a well-lit street, and I notice the buildings are getting smaller. A grin spreads across my face; we're getting closer. I never thought we'd get this far. Never thought we'd actually escape the soldiers who were pursuing us through the forest. My smile disappears. I still don't understand what happened to them. They just stopped following us.

A siren wails and my heart leaps into my throat. It's near.

We turn a corner, and I recognize the street—Finn's street!

Large houses, with gardens and lawns, line the road. The siren is getting closer. Liam jumps a low fence, and I follow him along the side of a house and to the backyard. We stick to the shadows as we make our way over fences and through gardens toward Finn's. I only hope those enforcers aren't in pursuit of us. From what Liam says, we're going to have enough to contend with when we reach Finn's.

He slows. The rest of us find our own shadows to wait in. With a quick glance back to make sure the others are no longer following him, he turns away from Finn's fence and jumps another one. I pull myself over and follow.

We move along the outside of Finn's back brick fence. Reaching out with my new senses, I try to tell whether there are any soldiers nearby, but as usual, since I've been in Hollowcrest, all I can discern is Liam beside me and then an ocean of energy. Even my friend's familiar signatures have been swallowed up now that I've moved away from them.

It doesn't matter. Liam crouches in the shadow of a shed and points to where a soldier is perched in a tree, watching Finn's house. I pull gently at the man's energy. I don't want to drain everyone in the neighborhood. I wince when he hits the ground with a thud, but Liam is already moving.

We jump another fence and continue circling Finn's property until Liam stops again and points out another soldier. I draw on his energy as well, hoping he's wedged in well enough to stay in his tree. It's going to be pretty suspicious that they both managed to fall asleep at the same time, but, at least not as suspicious as it would be if they had their throats slit. Liam reckons none of them will admit they fell asleep on watch anyway, not if they want to live. The army has no use for incompetence.

We only find one more soldier before circling back around to the others. We leave the church building and front of Finn's property. Better to sneak in through the back than to knock out more soldiers than necessary.

When we get back to the others, Liam gestures for us to all follow him and disappears over the high wall into Finn's garden.

I help boost the others over until I'm the only one left. Then, finding cracks in the bricks, scramble up and over after them. Only Liam waits for me. He points in two directions, and I notice the small red lights in the trees that betray cameras.

They're aimed at the back of his house and one side. I presume there are other cameras at the front and the other side. I frown. How are we going to reach the house undetected?

Liam points to the house, and I follow his aim to the back side window on the top floor. Looking at the camera, I try to tell whether it takes in that window or not, but there's no way for me to know.

"Sloppy work," murmurs Liam, and I take that to mean he can somehow tell that the window is not within the camera's range. I nod and start creeping through the shadows that line all the bushes. I'm glad Finn got to keep his overgrown garden. I bet Carlos didn't like that, but Liam reckoned he was going to have to keep his surveillance subtle.

I pass my friends, hidden between and underneath bushes. It's best for me and Liam to go first. Although, I know Finn would welcome all of them even if I wasn't here, there'll be less explaining to do if we go first. Looking at that wall, I decide it will be best for me to go first. I'm not even sure if Liam's fingers will fit between the cracks in the bricks.

When we reach the house, I climb onto Liam's shoulders. I could do it without his help, but this will give me a head start, and the sooner we all get in the house, the better. I'm trusting there's no surveillance inside.

The window is locked. I quietly rap my knuckles against the glass. If someone isn't in the room there's no chance of them hearing but, I don't want to draw attention from the soldier, who's likely hidden around the front, by making too much noise.

Pressing my palms flat against the glass, I try jerking it up and down. It gives a bit but not enough to make me think the latch is going to break. I pull the file from my pocket that I brought for just this purpose. Not that I knew I'd be breaking into Finn's but there's often somewhere to break into in a city.

I concentrate on maneuvering the file in the lock, but Finn's locks are a lot newer than anything in The City. "If Drimmy were here, he could do this easily," I mumble.

As if my words summon him, the curtain pulls aside, and a small black-haired boy peers out at me. A huge grin splits my face.

"Sample!" he yells.

I put my finger to my mouth, and he nods as he fumbles with the latch. Within moments, the window is open, and he's pulling me inside. He's not strong enough to hold me up though. He jumps out of the way as I land on the floor. A moment later, he's on top of me, wrapping his small arms around me.

Laughing, I roll over and return the hug. Liam climbs through the window and steps around our legs.

"Hi Number," says Drimmy, much more quietly but almost as warmly.

"Sample! What are you doing here?" Ollie greets me from the doorway.

"It's good to see you too," I reply.

I stand and Ollie wraps me in a hug. I melt into him. I'm home.

"I thought you were away and safe. It's not safe here Sample. They've got the house under surveillance, and if you had any idea what's happening in The City."

"They've started already?"

He nods. "On a small scale, but they're gearing up to go all out any day now."

"We've got to stop it!" I exclaim.

251

He nods. "That's what we've been discussing. You'd better come downstairs. I want to hear what you know, and we'll tell you what we've seen. Dominko has a lot of fresh intelligence too."

"Dominko! He's here?" I ask. Liam turns to look at me from where he's pulling someone up with a rope at the window. I can't read what his expression means, but I'm half out the door now and Finn calls me from the top of his stairs.

I fly down the hall to him and into his waiting arms. Oh, I've missed my old friends so much.

"Seriously! Does it really take both of you to investigate why the boy is so long at the toilet? We've work to do!" The words sound so strange coming from Dominko's mouth that I burst out laughing.

His head jerks toward me where I'm descending the stairs. "Sample! Can it really be you? I didn't think to ever see you again. You're a vision." He sweeps me into his arms and I can't stop laughing. Who speaks like that?

When I manage to disengage myself, I say, "It's good to see you too Dominko."

"And that soldier? Is he with you still? Did he manage to keep his hands off you?"

I laugh again. "He did too well. You should be more concerned about whether I kept my hands off him."

"That dirty thing? You wouldn't? He has no dress sense at all."

"Last you saw, he was wearing his uniform."

"Exactly."

I eye Dominko's pink silk shirt and he preens. "You like?" he asks.

I can't help but shake my head.

He waves his hand, "It's hardly important anyway. Have you heard what's happening in The City?" he asks as he returns to his seat. He doesn't make it there. Liam is standing like a wall between him and the lounge. Dominko is tall but he still has to look up to meet Liam's eyes.

"I thought you said you two had an understanding?" Liam growls.

Dominko takes a step back. "We do," he replies.

"That didn't look like the reunion of people who love each other."

"We do. It's just unspoken though. But, I do," he says with a large smile, "And of course she loves me. I mean, who wouldn't?" he asks with a wave to display his body.

I cock my head. What on earth are they talking about?

"That is not an understanding. That is just an enormously inflated ego," Liam's growl is fierce now, and Dominko is starting to look nervous but not as much as I think he should be. Liam's face looks like a tornado about to hit.

Dominko takes another step back. "Well, haven't you asked her? She can speak for herself."

They both turn to face me. The room is filling with our friends as they come down the stairs, and I turn to see how they like the place, but I can feel both Liam and Dominko's gazes still on me. I turn back to them.

"What?"

"Well, my darling. What say you? Do you love me?" Dominko asks.

I crack up laughing, but instead of joining in, his smile falters. "That is not a very flattering way to respond," he says.

I screw my face up. He's not serious. He starts to fidget and moves farther away from Liam.

"You're joking," I say.

"My father forced me to get engaged to another. You must understand, I thought I'd never see you again, but now that you're back, everything will be different. This time we'll have time to plan and it will be me that runs away with you."

I can't help but smile at the thought of Dominko surviving in the mountains and going through everything I've been through with Liam.

"See! The thought makes you happy!"

I gently shake my head. "No, Dominko. I'm sorry, but it is not to be."

"You got engaged to another!" Liam's tone is controlled, but the fury behind it makes even me take a step back. "After telling me you had an understanding!"

"Umm yes, but I don't love Francesca. She bores me to tears, quite frankly. But, why does it matter? It's not like she'd ever be interested in you anyway. I did you a favor by keeping your expectations low. Face it man, after all the time you've been together, if you were meant for each other, you wouldn't have let me stand in your way."

"Fool man!" says Liam, turning his back on Dominko and heading for the kitchen in the back of the house. I can't tell whether his words are meant for Dominko. He almost seemed to be abusing himself.

I watch him go with a frown. What was all that about? I'm not entirely sure, but I do know a small slither of hope has taken root in my gut. If we survive all this, I'm going to make sure we get the time alone together for me to find out.

"You've lost weight," Dominko's disapproving voice breaks my reverie. "I forgot how skinny you are."

I roll my eyes at him. "You haven't changed a bit."

His hands go to his chest and a smile lights his face. He inclines his head and replies, "Well, of course not."

"Ahem," interrupts Ollie. "As wonderful as it is to have Sample back, we do need to get back to planning."

"Yeah, good luck getting any sense out of Dominko now. Sample walks in the room and he turns back into a dandy," says Drimmy.

Dominko shoots Drimmy a dark look and sits down. "Getting back to planning would suggest we'd started. But, all we've done is lay out all the problems. He's just too powerful to stop."

"Who is?" I ask.

Dominko averts his eyes. When he doesn't answer, I look to Ollie, Drimmy, and Finn for a reply, but they're all looking at Dominko.

The only sound is of chairs scraping on the wooden floor as people shuffle into seats.

"While Drimmy and I have been going into The City to investigate the progress of the harvesting operation there, Dominko has been doing a lot of investigating and discovered who's behind the operation."

Chapter 31

"You've been to The City! The family?" I ask.

Ollie's shoulders fall. "Jerle and Samantha were lost in the cull," he replies.

A sharp pain stabs through my chest and doesn't let up. My hand flies to my mouth as if it can somehow stifle my grief. "No," I whisper.

Liam walks back into the room with a full flask of water which he hands to Adam. "Fill us in on what you know about the planned harvest of clones in The City," he says.

No one answers.

"What did I miss?" Liam asks.

"Two of Sample's friends were killed in a cull," Adam murmurs to him before passing the flask on to Darla.

Liam's eyes fill with compassion, and he takes a step toward me. I wish he'd keep coming, but he doesn't.

"There'll be a lot more dead if we don't work out how to stop this harvesting. You should see how many tables they've prepared for it," says Drimmy.

"You've seen it?" Jake asks.

Drimmy nods.

"Aye, we've seen it," replies Dominko.

"You've seen it?" I ask. "But I thought it was in The City."

"It is. I've been there twice now."

Despite my grief, I can't help smiling at the thought of Dominko in The City.

"What on earth could have convinced you to go to The City?" I ask.

His shoulders slump. "The first time was to find someone who knew about the engineering of the healing clones."

My eyes widen in interest, but he waves me away.

"But that's another story altogether, though it did lead to some of my first suspicions. The second time was to investigate a conversation I'd overheard about harvesting." He takes a deep breath. "I've spent the last couple of months digging up all I can on the operation and my father. I've bugged all his devices and searched his entire computer history and all his accounts. It's my father who's running the operation."

My jaw drops. Dominko's father? I mean I knew the man was mean, but he's Dominko's father? It's difficult to believe he could be that evil. Poor Dominko. Now I can recognize the look on his face for shame.

"So you came here?" I ask.

He nods. "I got here yesterday. I've researched all I can, but I still don't know how to stop him."

I feel the blood drain from my face. "He's got the whole army behind him."

Dominko nods.

"He's just one man. We don't need to face the army. We'll get to him when they're not around," says Liam.

"Too late for that," says Drimmy.

Finn nods. "He holed himself up in the compound yesterday. He's recalled soldiers from everywhere. All the gates are closed. The walls are high and electrified."

"Dominko can ..."

Dominko is shaking his head at me. "I tried to lose my tail and clear any tracking devices he had on me, but by now, he knows I'm here. I've never had access to the army, and he won't be letting me in now."

"We'll just wait him out. He can't stay in there forever, can he?" Carla asks.

"Harvesting starts in two days if he doesn't bring it forward. Something has spooked him. It's weird how he suddenly took fright," says Ollie.

Dominko nods. "He's got a hovter ready to fly him out with the first shipment of organs in two night's time."

I bite my lip. Harvesting in two days! That's too soon! It only gives us one day to stop him. I look around at my friends. They're all exhausted. I've fed them all my surplus energy over the last few days and with the soldiers no longer following us, I haven't been able to get any more.

"Tell us what you do know Dominko, not what you can't do," I glance at Liam. His tone is not one I'm used to hearing from him. He's more angry with Dominko than I've ever seen him.

Dominko spreads his hands, palms up. "I know he's in charge. I know he's got most of the people in Hollowcrest with power behind him. Though few want to be there. They are following him out of fear for the most part. He's threatened to ruin anyone who doesn't comply with him. And if financial and business threats weren't enough, he's blackmailed them." Dominko pauses and, lowering his eyes, says, "In two cases, I discovered threats against people's children."

"We can use that," says Jake.

"I did approach a couple of people, but they won't work against him. No one has any hope of succeeding, and everyone is too afraid of father finding out about them to work together. They said they will support me if I can overthrow him, but that's the most I could get out of them."

I shake my head.

"We've always known we were up against someone with power. We just need to work out how to get to him," says Liam.

"But even if we do miraculously get to him, he's got the army with him," says Brody.

"Well, obviously we won't confront them head-on. We've got to think of something else," says Liam.

"We've got to try," I agree.

"Well duh. I didn't come all this way to not even have a bit of a fight," says Carla.

Dominko is looking thoughtful. It's a strange expression on his face. He's different than he used to be. I'm still surprised he's here trying to take on his father. It must have been a shock to find out what his father's doing, though I'm not sure the Dominko I first met would have thought there was anything wrong with it. I wonder what changed him.

He pulls out a device, taps on it and a hologram fills the room. We all shuffle back to try to get a better look. It just looks like a big box.

"The army compound," says Liam.

"Daddy dear—" Dominko's mouth puckers in distaste. "Carlos has blocked my access to any of the security systems associated with the compound. I've been trying to break in, but he hasn't used any of his usual signatures. I've never seen anything locked down so tight. He must have had this planned as a backup for a long time. I never knew he was so paranoid. This isn't an overnight security system. He must have thought for a long time that a situation might arise where he would have to be locked away safely; and in all his plans, he decided he wouldn't want to include me in his emergency strategies."

Silence fills the room. I shuffle my feet and turn my attention back to the hologram. I wish I could understand what I'm looking at. Blue lines crisscross each other forming a big rectangle.

Dominko shakes his head. "There's nothing."

"What about that?" says Connor pointing at a small box at the base of the hologram.

Dominko shakes his head. "It's just the water pipes. They're too small."

"How small?" asks Paige eyeing me up and down.

Dominko looks over at me with interest before looking away again. "You'd have to be half her size to squeeze in." He zooms in to reveal a pipe that twists and breaks off into a number of smaller pipes. "See here," he points to where the pipe winds in a sharp, angled 'S'. "She's too tall to maneuver her body around these bends. She'd have to be a contortionist."

"I could do it," says Drimmy.

"No," I reply.

"Shut it Sample," he replies. "I can do it."

"And then what will you do when you get in there? You can't take on the army by yourself," says Finn.

"I'm not stupid. Once I get in there, I'll let the rest of yers in; same as Sample would if she went."

Ollie cuffs him. "Don't talk to Finn like that."

Drimmy moves away from Ollie and draws closer to the hologram of the pipes. "I can do it."

"You can't do it on your own. I can turn the main supply of water off, but that will only take you to here," he points at a spot just inside the main wall. I can see another wall just inside it. "Once there, you'd need someone to exit the pipes and divert the water already in there while you went through this "S" bend, and then there are computer codes that would need to be entered here to open these valves while this section is off or you'll never get through to the next section." Dominko shakes his head. "No, you'd need at least eight people to pull this off."

"I can jump in and out to do what needs to be done," protests Drimmy.

"No, you can't!" Dominko raises his voice. "Once you leave half of the controls, they will revert to their default, they can't be unattended. It requires a team; not just one person. And even if you could, there just wouldn't be enough time. Once I turn the water off, the whole thing will be a race before you're discovered."

"It's not going to work," says Jake. "We need to stop wasting time and look at other options."

My shoulders sag. He's right. We won't be getting in through there.

We stare at the hologram Dominko's expanded in silence. It's beginning to make a bit of sense to me, but I can't see any other entry points.

"You're supposed to be the tech genius," says Liam. "You'll need to find a way to shut it down."

Dominko punches his knee. "I've been trying!" He jumps to his feet and stalks to the edge of the room where I see a desk set up with a couple of computers. I've never seen anything like them but Dominko sits down in front of them, and his hands fly as he pulls up different images and scrolls through pages of code.

My eyes go back to the hologram, and I continue looking for something we might have missed. Everyone else does the same until Finn interrupts us with a call to eat.

Only then do the delectable smells of stew and fresh vegetables reach me. With groans of exhaustion, my friends force themselves to their feet, and we head for the kitchen.

We feast on the hot food before Finn manages to send us upstairs, with arms full of clean blankets, to find places to sleep. I want to protest but I'm not coming up with anything just staring at the confusing hologram. I don't even know what most of the thin blue lines represent and Dominko doesn't have the time to explain them to me. I look around at my friend's faces. They're in no shape to take on Carlos and the army, as if they ever could anyway. I can't deny, we all need sleep. Maybe we'll be able to come up with some better ideas in the morning.

Chapter 32

"Sample, we need you," Liam's strong hand is shaking my shoulder; I begin to emerge from the deepest sleep I've had in weeks.

"It would be so much more romantic if you didn't say we," I murmur.

His hand stops shaking me, and I crack my eyes open to see how he responds to my crazy words.

He's smiling. It's the first time I've seen a smile from him in a week; since he killed all the unconscious soldiers. I've been worried about him but had no idea how to help him. Maybe all he needs is to have his ego stroked; though, after his bizarre argument with Dominko, dare I hope I mean more to him?

I'm blissfully aware of his hand still resting on my shoulder, and I could melt into his eyes.

"What's taking you so long?" Ollie's loud whisper breaks the moment.

Liam takes a deep breath and with one lithe movement is at the door. With a sigh, I follow him—a lot less gracefully.

Liam slides down the stair rail, reaching the common room below in just a moment. I raise an eyebrow at his uncharacteristic display and follow in a much more dignified manner. Or at least, it would be dignified if my sleepy feet didn't keep tripping over the blanket I've got wrapped around me.

"What's up?" I ask when I reach the room. My eyes lift to take in the most beautiful woman I've ever seen. "Bianka!" I exclaim, hurtling myself forward into her arms.

"She says she's brought some little people," murmurs Dominko. He's looking at me, then at his computer. He even takes a turn looking at the ceiling. I can't help but smile. I've never seen Dominko look uncomfortable around a woman before. But then, Bianka has that effect on everyone. My eyes dart to Liam. He's watching me, still with that small smile from upstairs. What has gotten into the man?

"They said they know you," Bianka purrs. Dominko leaves us to go to his computers; by the bags under his eyes, I'm guessing he hasn't slept in days. Certainly not in the two nights since we've been here. I'm surprised I finally managed to nod off. No matter how hard we try, we can't think of a way to get to Carlos and so the best we've been able to come up with is a war in The City against the scientists. We know we won't last long or achieve much though, not with the soldiers on their side. If we can't get rid of Carlos, we won't be able to stop the harvesting.

"I don't understand," I say to Bianka. "You brought them here from The City? How did you get through?"

"Oh," she waves an elegant hand. "I came through one of the gates the scientists use. But, they're not from The City. They somehow managed to crawl through the wheat fields under cover of darkness and got past the drones into The City. They've apparently been crawling through buildings for days looking for you."

"Looking for me? But who? Where are they from?" I ask.

"I don't know. They said you were friends. Did I do wrong to bring them here?" Bianka looks around with a cute worry line between her eyes that does nothing to mar her beauty.

"What is your sense of them?" Finn asks. "Do you think they could be working for Carlos?"

"Oh, I wouldn't think so. They're rough, but they're certainly not soldiers. Though I guess, they would be good as spies. You know, as they could get into such small spaces."

"Wait! How big are they?" I ask.

"They're tiny!" Bianka giggles and holds her hand at hip height to show me their height.

"The little people!" I exclaim to Liam.

"How did they get here?" he asks me at the same time.

"Where are they?" I ask Bianka.

"At Marg's. I couldn't risk trying to bring them here. The soldiers know Ollie and Drimmy live here. Dominko was able to create covers for them. And Ollie sometimes gets a visit from a sex clone," she says with a suggestive sway of her hips and a giggle.

Ollie clears his throat in protest, and his cheeks redden.

"It would have been hard to come up with a cover for so many tiny clones though. Luckily, they haven't thought it necessary to watch Marg's."

Liam gives a small irritated shake of his head. I find it amusing that he takes it as a personal insult whenever the army shows incompetence.

"I told them you could render the soldiers unconscious so we could smuggle our visitors in. I didn't realize it was our friends," he adds.

I raise an eyebrow at him.

"Your friends," he amends, his smile fading.

I rest a comforting hand on his arm. He's done much over the last few months to protect us that he can't be proud of.

"Well, where are the soldiers you want me to render unconscious?" I ask.

"Not yet, Sample," says Finn. "Bianka will need to go back to Marg's to ready them and bring them here, but she needs to visit with Ollie for at least an hour before she can leave."

Ollie's look of shock at Finn's words cause a bark of laughter to erupt from me.

"It's so good to see you, Sample. We've been so worried about you. I can't tell you how happy we all were when the tiny clones told us they'd been living with you in safety. Come," she takes my hand and begins pulling me toward the kitchen. "Let's get tea."

Despite how good it is to see Bianka and sit and talk with her, Ollie, Finn, and Drimmy; my mind can't rest. I try to still my bobbing knees repeatedly, but I want the little people safe here at Finn's, and even more of a stress is my worry about the cloning that is scheduled to begin tomorrow.

Despite my impatience, I still haven't heard everything I want to know about my family in The City when Finn informs us it's time for her to go. She slips out the front door with a flirtatious giggle meant for the soldier's ears and then disappears into the night.

I pace the front room until Liam takes me back out the upstairs window and via a circuitous route past three guards, who get another unexpected doze during their watch, around to the front of Finn's where I draw the energy from another two soldiers guarding the front of Finn's house and the church building.

Then, Liam takes one of the smelly, black balloons he's been working on in Finn's kitchen and throws it into the air. I watch as it sails toward a tree and explodes against a camera, leaving a sticky mess of goo all over the lens. He takes a few steps through the shadows next to a high unshapen hedge and pelts another balloon at a second camera. I can see he has a spare balloon, but he doesn't need it. His first two shots did their job.

With the guards and cameras out of commission, we sprint toward the street. I hate the thought of the little people wandering the streets of Hollowcrest with no protection.

Liam stops me at the front hedge and peers out along the road. When he's satisfied it's all clear, we run toward

Marg's, sticking close to the low fences for what little cover they offer.

We don't get far before I notice Bianka hurrying back toward us.

"Where are they?" I ask in dismay.

"They're there," Liam's voice is low, reminding me to moderate mine.

I look around, but they're clearly not there.

He points toward a low brick fence near Bianka. I hurry forward, but I can't see anything of my friends. I'm stopped next to a small open gate and almost jump out of my skin when something slides into my hand.

I manage to stifle a scream and look down to see Kayana smiling up at me, her face barely visible in the darkness.

My held breath explodes out of me.

"It's really you! You've gotten way too good at creeping around."

"We've had lots of practice over the last few months."

I think of all the farms we've raided together and have to resist the urge to pick her up and squeeze her. The adults don't take kindly to that.

"We have to get inside," Liam says.

Kayana scowls at him, but we all turn and rush back to Finn's.

Chapter 33

When we get back, I can't contain my excitement any longer and get down on my knees and hug each of the eighteen adults and teenagers who've followed me here. Now that we're inside, excited high-pitched voices fill the air.

"I'm trying to concentrate here," Dominko exclaims, rising from his chair. A look of confusion passes over his face as he notices the little people for the first time.

"What are those?" he asks.

My jaw drops.

Gollum raises himself up to his full height, puffing out his slender chest. "We are tunnel clones," he announces. "Or more recently," he adds with a wink for me, "little people."

"Yes you are. You are! And you are exactly what we need!" He punches the air in triumph.

"You really need to get some sleep," I tell him.

"This is it," he exclaims gesturing at the little people. "They can get through the water tunnel. They can get us to Carlos!"

"No!" I reply.

"What are you talking about 'no'? Sample, don't you see? It's the only way. I've been working for days and I—can't—crack—the security."

"They're not doing it," I reply in a voice that refuses to let down.

Dominko's shoulders sag. "Then it will be war because, without them, we don't get to Carlos."

"Your father," I spit.

He scowls at me, and I regret the jab, but I won't let anyone threaten the safety of the little people. I rescued them, and I've been protecting them for months, and I can't let them just walk into something as dangerous as the army compound.

"What does he want us to do?" Gollum asks.

"Nothing. You must be tired," I reply.

"Well yes, we've been pushing ourselves relentlessly to try to get here to help you. Father Bayle drove us a good distance in a bus though, so we got to rest then. Yes, we're tired, but we will not sleep now. You know we don't sleep at night."

"Well, you must be hungry. Let's get you to the kitchen," I say, waving them in that direction with my arms and trying to usher them out of the room and away from Dominko.

"Let's," Gollum replies in a firm voice, "hear what it is you need for us to do."

"It's nothing. We'll find another way."

"There is no other way," says Dominko.

"Sample," Liam reaches out a hand to my arm. Gollum glares at him. Liam ignores him and with eyes only for me, says gently, "Let Dominko talk to them."

"It's too dangerous."

"We will decide what is too dangerous for us, child," says Gollum, reminding me he has at least ten years on me despite the fact I tower over him. My shoulders sag.

I leave the room in protest but only get as far as the kitchen where I set about preparing a meal for the little people. Despite my withdrawal, I keep my ears peeled to hear everything Dominko says to them.

As I cook, I continue to formulate objections and look for any opportunity to argue with what Dominko says to them. I can't come up with any new arguments though. None other than, I don't want them going into danger. But they've come all this way to help me. My eyes tear at their loyalty. Despite my objections, Dominko's plan is a good one, and unless I want a war we can't win, there doesn't seem to be another alternative.

I crouch amongst the trees outside the soldier compound, staring across the wide empty expanse that separates me from a tall electrified wall. Behind that lies the army—clones designed as killing machines with enhanced abilities and no respect for life, answerable only to Carlos Dahlquist.

Carlos, who is my goal. He has to be stopped. He has perpetrated enough atrocities against clones, and his treatment of us cannot be allowed to continue. If we don't stop him then harvesting in The City will begin in only a few hours and the unviables who have always struggled to survive will be reduced to nothing but farm stock ready for slaughter.

My friends, my little friends, are also behind that wall. My lip is bleeding from where I keep worrying at it with my teeth. So much could go wrong. I keep glancing at Dominko. He's got them commed and is in constant contact with them. He stopped giving me updates almost an hour ago. He's pretending I'm not here, and I'm trying not to distract him from the device he holds and the instructions he's relaying to the little people inside the walls of the compound.

My fingers start rapping against my knee again, and Liam takes my hand in his. It's not much comfort at the moment. A little hand-holding isn't going to keep my friends alive.

"Yes!" murmurs Dominko.

I look at him expectantly, but he's typing furiously on his small touch screen.

"Get ready," he murmurs without lifting his eyes.

Liam gestures wide enough for everyone hidden in the trees to see him.

The worry lines above his eyes are visible even in the dark. It's hard enough for him leading the clones from the Resistance, who he's trained, into dangerous situations, but many from The City have also joined us and couldn't be convinced not to.

Ollie and Drimmy have been recruiting for this battle for some time, and there are a lot of unviables who are determined to fight for their right to be more than just discarded mistakes.

Liam has spent the last two hours trying to work out how to place them so they'll be in the least danger possible, but in the end, they'll be in the most vulnerable situation. They are to serve as a distraction so we can get to Carlos.

"Now!" says Dominko.

We rise to our feet and sprint from the trees toward the gate. Close to one hundred clones follow us, not as quiet on the grass and sticks as they usually move in The City.

I'm still fifty meters from the wall when I start drawing energy, rendering all the guards unconscious.

When we reach the gate, Dominko gives it a push, and it slides open. He sighs out in relief.

We pause just inside the gate.

"What happened to the guards?" he asks. I frown at him until I realize he doesn't know about my new ability and was too busy on his computer when we talked about me downing the guards. Liam is pointing groups of people in different directions. Even with the closest guards down, we're trying to be quiet. There's no time to catch Dominko up now; Liam leads me, Dominko, and the others from the Resistance in another direction. We weave through buildings, while Dominko uses his device to unlock section after section. Whatever he got the little people to do seems to have given him access to all the systems within the compound.

With Liam's knowledge of the base and Dominko's hacking skills and knowledge of his father, I'm sure we'll find Carlos wherever he's hiding in this warren. I can't say I'm excited, but adrenaline is pumping through me. We're going to do this! Carlos will be stopped, and my family will be safe.

After an hour of searching, my confidence has fled. The compound is deserted. Well, at least, it looks deserted. My senses are still confused by a massive amount of life energy, but no matter where we search, we can't find anyone. By all appearances, Carlos has fled and taken the army with him.

I still can't understand what has him so spooked though. Even if he knew we were onto him, what could he have to fear from less than one hundred unviables when he has the army?

Liam stops, and I come to an abrupt halt behind him.

"We haven't heard any gunfire at all," he says.

I nod. It's been the only thing comforting me, knowing my friends and family haven't been shot.

He starts walking toward a door. "They'll be in the training area," he says.

"In the middle of the night?" I ask.

"It's the only place we haven't looked. I sent the others there because I thought they'd be safe there, but it's impossible that *no one* would have discovered them. If we haven't heard any gunfire, it means they've already been captured."

My stomach heaves.

"Faster," I push him in the back, urging him forward.

As we sprint toward the training area, I become aware of a wall of energy in front of me. Liam's right. All the soldiers are congregated there. Why couldn't I have figured that out sooner? Who knows what's happened to my friends while we've been searching the whole compound?

Now that we're out of the buildings, I notice the night has grown lighter. My belly clenches. It can't be dawn yet! We have to find Carlos before they start cutting open clones. They've probably already caught the first lot of sacrifices.

We round a corner, and it grows even lighter ahead. As we race forward, I realize huge lights are lighting up the area.

Dismay fills me as the soldiers come into sight. There are hundreds of them. I've never seen so many people in one place before. There are probably more than hundreds. Thousands, if Liam and Dominko are to be believed. I have no reason to doubt them; I've never seen so many people before, not even at Carnaval.

We slow to a stop before we reach them and Liam waves us off in two directions. I don't move. What's the point? We can't fight this many soldiers. This was always supposed to be a covert mission. We were supposed to sneak past the soldiers to get to Carlos, not fight them.

There's a voice coming through some speakers. I recognize the smug tones of Carlos. All but a few soldiers who are standing peering into the shadows, obviously on guard, are facing in the one direction. That is where Carlos will be.

My feet glide forward of their own volition. We cannot fight the soldiers, but I will talk to Carlos. If we can't stop him with a gun, then I will try to stop him with words. There's no point retreating now. I've come this far; I'm not leaving without trying.

Liam has slipped off to the side with the others and hasn't noticed I'm not following. He'll be furious with me, but that probably doesn't matter. I won't be around to worry about it.

Chapter 34

"Let her through," Carlos' voice grates through a microphone. Soldiers step back, creating a pathway for me to walk along. I reach a wide empty circle around a small podium on which Carlos stands.

"Don't come any closer," orders Carlos. I ignore him. I need to be closer to him. I need to see his eyes. I need for him to see mine. Not to see their color, but so he can see my sincerity—so I can persuade him. I can't influence someone I can't see clearly.

"So, here's the unviable who's been killing my soldiers."

My chin jerks up. I want to deny his accusation. I never killed anyone. But I know that's not true. I'm just as much to blame as anyone. If it wasn't for me, the others never would have been in a position to kill so many.

"What makes you think it was me?" I ask instead. How does he even know I was there?

He laughs. It's an angry laugh, with no humor in it. So different to Dominko's. "How many of your type do you think there are walking around?" he asks.

"I said stop!" he yells.

I can hear thousands of guns being aimed at me. I do what he wants. I can see him clearly now. His features are so similar to Dominko's. His jaw is strong, his cheekbones high, and his lips full. He even has Dominko's blue eyes and thick lashes. His eyes are so like Dominko's and yet so different. There is none of Dominko's kindness or good humor. Instead, I see a calculating glare full of hatred, bitterness, and thinly veiled fear.

My brow creases.

"What are you afraid of Carlos?" I ask.

"I'm not afraid. I don't know how you got in here. But you can't hurt me."

"I haven't come here to hurt you. I just want to talk to you."

"Ha!" I resist blocking my ears as his insincere laugh bursts through the speakers. "I know what you want. You want to kill me. I control the clones, and you want your revenge. I always knew this day would come. Knew you would rise up against me. I thought there'd be more of you though," he looks nervously toward the buildings and then, with a glance at his soldiers, seems to discount his worry. "I thought I'd gotten rid of your kind though. None of you were supposed to survive."

His words feel like a kick to my gut. "What did you do?" I whisper. My voice grows in strength. "Why would you want to get rid of healing clones?"

"Healing clones," he spits the words at me. "Killing clones is what you should be called. People worry about the army, but you're the one they should be worried about. Falisco, with all his high ideals and moral concerns about engineering soldiers, and then he made you!"

"I help people," my voice sounds weak in my own ears. Where does his hate come from? I straighten my shoulders. I will not bow under his condemnation. "I'm not a soldier, engineered to kill. I'm a healer, a giver of life."

"Giver of life?" Carlos' roar is incredulous. "How can you give something you don't contain? You're just a clone … and an unviable at that. You're worthless; you don't even know what it means to be alive. You don't have a soul. You don't know what it means to be a person. You don't know what makes us tick, what it feels like to have humanity coursing through your veins, to be truly human. You are just an imitation, a tool. You were made for our use; that is all. You can't give life when you don't even know what life feels like."

I take a step toward him, and he stumbles backward; a small surge of satisfaction fills me. His words remind me of the abuse I received as a child. I believed them for most of my life. But, no more.

"You can't hurt me. My soldiers will shoot you as soon as I give the command. You are nothing but a weak, untrained, failed tool. You cannot succeed against me. I am too strong for you, I have too much power at my command." He gestures to the soldiers. "My power will squash you. You are insignificant, and no one will miss you. You are dirt, and my power will sweep you away."

"Your power?" I ask. He nods, suddenly unsure in the face of my calm answer.

"I am not weak; I am not nothing. I am something, someone. I have worth, and you are wrong. I would be missed. I do know what it is to be human, to love and be loved. And I know better than you what it is to have life coursing through my veins. I have had more life flowing through me than you could ever conceive. I would be missed, but I won't be," my voice is growing louder and stronger. His words have woken a wild fury in me. I will not accept that kind of abuse any longer. "You speak of your power. You have no power." I fling my arm wide. "I am the power!" I shout.

The army collapses around me.

A wave of energy surges through me almost knocking me from my feet. I fight to catch my breath and find my balance. Even though I've closed my walls again after draining the soldiers, I can still feel waves and waves of energy washing over me.

Carlos quakes before me. "You can't," he stutters. "They told me, but it's not possible. You can't drain clones."

"Apparently, I can. Apparently, clones aren't as different from you as you have always led us to believe. I know that now, through and through. My body knows that—my energy knows that."

Carlos raises a gun at me. I draw on his energy, dropping him to his knees and rendering him so weak that his arm falls to his side and the gun hangs uselessly from his limp fingers.

"You have no moral compass. You are nothing," he sneers.

My body burns with energy and rage. This man has destroyed so many lives, killed so many children, robbed so many of their freedom. I advance on him, slowly pulling the energy from him. I want him to see me clearly as he dies.

His eyes are full of hate and fear, filling me with contempt.

As I reach him, he collapses to the ground. I can sense a small spark of life still within him. Sneering, I begin to snuff it out but hesitate. For some inexplicable reason, Finn's face swims before me. He wouldn't want me to do this. And

Father Bayle. A sense of peace passes over me as it always does when I remember his love and his prayer for me.

Carlos' words of abuse are meaningless in the face of such love. His life, no matter how foul is meaningful in the face of Finn's compassion. Their God, who has brought so much healing to my life, wouldn't want me to now discard Carlos'.

I take a step back and turning my back on him, search for my friends. There's no one; no one standing, that is. Bodies cover the ground in every direction. A wave of anguish washes over me, and I feel like vomiting, despite the overwhelming life and energy filling me.

Carlos was right to fear me. I can't believe I'm capable of causing so much devastation. The power surging through me terrifies me.

I look around for my friends again. I want them close. With them, I know who I am. I can't see them, but I walk back the way I came and circle around the mass of soldiers, searching for them.

I find Ollie first and seep some energy into him, careful not to let any stray elsewhere. The last thing I need is to wake any soldiers now. Who knows what they would do in the face of all their downed comrades.

Ollie leaps to his feet and stumbles from foot to foot, staring at the lifeless bodies covering the training ground. I'm grateful for his lack of speech. I don't know if I can explain what he's looking at.

I continue on, waking the others until I find Liam. Collapsing on the ground beside him, I leak him some energy. He sits up, surveys the field and then pulls me into his arms.

I sink against him and sob against his shoulder. There's still too much energy filling me. I have to contain it. If I let it go, we'll be slaughtered by the soldiers, but with no target left, no one to aim my anger at, I don't know what to do with the emotions roiling through me riding on the crest of the life filling me.

Liam lets me cry for a while, then pulls me to my feet and leads me to where Dominko lies sprawled on the floor. His face is lax, and there's a small line of drool dripping from his mouth, causing me to smile.

"He's ruined his shirt," I say to Liam.

He grunts. "As much as it pains me to say this, we need him awake."

Liam's still holding my hand. I lean against his arm, drawing comfort from him, as I leak energy to Dominko.

He bolts upright. "Are we dead?"

He leaps to his feet and spins in circles, mouth and eyes wide open, as he surveys the field of unconscious soldiers.

"Where's Carlos?" He asks in a high-pitched voice.

I point toward him, but Dominko's paying no attention to me. He hops from one foot to the other trying to see everywhere. "Where's Carlos?" he repeats.

I grab his arm and draw his attention, then point in the direction of Carlos again.

I know he can't see him, but he seems to calm somewhat. "What happened?" he whispers.

"You've had your head stuck in that computer so much you haven't caught up on Sample's new abilities," says Liam.

Dominko frowns and turns a questioning look on me.

With a small shrug, I say, "I've learned how to take in other's energy."

He shakes his head.

"But …"

His face clears as he looks around. "This is what my father was trying to prevent. That's why he shut down the healing clone project."

"He said, I should be called 'killing clone'." My voice hitches and Liam squeezes my hand.

"No," he murmurs. Dominko is surveying the field and doesn't voice an opinion. I square my shoulders against his judgment.

"Are they dead?" he asks.

"No!" I reply in shock. "Merely unconscious."

"It will not take them long to wake," Liam adds. "You need to position yourself to take over the army and Clone Industries before they and your father do wake."

With a deep breath, Dominko nods. He pulls out his phone and, dialing a number, stalks toward the podium. He doesn't get far before he has to slow and pick his way through the fallen bodies.

I just want to collapse in Liam's arms and never resurface, but I turn to find other friends and people from The City.

Liam sticks by my side as I search. I expect his help in finding people, but he seems preoccupied.

I'm still looking for the little people, when he says to me, "We should wake one soldier at a time and enlist them to support Dominko, so he doesn't have to contend with all of them en masse. If he has some behind him when the others wake, they will follow suit."

"I can't find the little people," I say.

"There will be plenty of time to find them, once we have the compound secured."

Tears fill my eyes. I've turned into a sodden mess. My gut churns with energy and the need to find my little friends, but Liam's right. We need to close this deal; it could still easily fall to pieces.

The soldier's health regenerates so quickly, it might not be long before they wake and I don't think I could survive taking in any more energy. As it is, I feel like I might float away at any moment. It's only Liam's presence that's helping me to stay aware of my surroundings, rather than disappearing into the euphoric buzz of energy bouncing around inside me.

Liam leads me toward Dominko where he proceeds to outline a plan and suggest the best Numbers to fall into line under Dominko's new reign. Dominko says something about 'powers that be' being on their way, but I'm not really listening. I'm looking over the field of bodies.

A burning desire to heal them consumes me, and I take a step toward the closest body.

"Sample. Sample." I can hear Liam's voice, but it's just a buzzing.

"Sample!" He grabs me and spins me toward him. Taking my two cheeks between his hands, he stares into my eyes. His features swim before me.

"I've got to heal them," I slur.

"Sample! Focus on me!" He's yelling at me, but I don't know why.

He leans forward, and his lips meet mine. His kiss is firm, and within a moment, he's not holding my cheeks anymore but has his arms wrapped around me and his body pressed against mine. I become aware of his hard muscles first, and then, as I realize what is happening, I begin to kiss him back.

When he pulls away from me, he searches my eyes.

"Mmm, that was nice," I smile at him. "What took you so long?"

He doesn't smile back. "Are you alright now?" he asks.

My own smile falters. I nod in reply, and he turns away from me.

I want to crumple to the ground, but pride keeps me on my feet. I turn away from him and notice the wall of soldiers aiming guns at us only meters away. There are easily one hundred of them.

Chapter 35

I groan. I must have given the soldiers energy.

"Lower your weapons," I hear Dominko say through the speakers. The soldiers look up in confusion. Their eyes pass from Dominko to his fallen father to the mass of grounded soldiers around them.

"Everything is under control. We have reached an agreement. I am in control while my father is incapacitated. I won't ask again. Lower your weapons." Dominko's voice grates on my nerves. Where did this authoritative manner come from? He sounds more like his father than the Dominko I know. A shudder races through me. Have we just replaced one power-hungry Dahlquist for another?

The soldiers lower their guns, and Dominko continues to give them instructions. There is to be a meeting between all of Hollowcrest's most influential business people, and he expects the soldiers to provide security for them. He offers promotions for those who show themselves the most useful and requests volunteers to brief the other soldiers as they wake.

I hop from foot to foot, itching to heal more people, but fighting the urge with all my might. I don't need the humiliation of forcing Liam to kiss me again.

Dominko seems to be talking in slow motion. I scan the other side of the training ground wondering if the little people are over there somewhere. Surely I could be looking for them while Dominko gets the soldiers prepared for me to wake more of them.

I don't want to ask Liam to help me find them though; I can't even make eye contact with him. Neither am I game to leave his side. As much as I hate to admit it, he's the only thing keeping me grounded. Even without looking at him, I'm always aware of him when he's nearby; now more than ever.

He tries to take my hand, but I pull away and use my fingers to pinch my arm instead. I can hardly feel my nails digging in, no matter how deep I sink them in. All I can feel is health and vigor.

Dominko's voice stops droning, and I realize he's looking at me. I let out a sigh. Finally!

"Who?" I ask. He gestures behind me, and I see about fifty soldiers stationed around the field.

"Just wake ten at a time," he says.

As if it's that easy. My energy is bursting against my walls, threatening to brim over the top and carry me away with it. I don't think I can control it enough to wake ten at a time. Reaching the group, I kneel beside a soldier and, taking his hand, direct a tiny bit of energy toward him. It's easier to do it that way. I scan the field. It's going to take a long time but it's the safest way at the moment. Maybe when I've depleted some of my stores, I'll be able to do it more quickly.

I work through the field until dawn, but I never tire. Another soldier leaps to his feet before me and is quickly briefed by one of the volunteers who have followed me around tirelessly doing their duty.

I search for another body, but all I can see is ranks and ranks of soldiers. They started waking of their own accord a while ago, and it seems the last of them has risen. I'm still brimming with energy though, and with everyone around me in perfect health, the power refuses to leave me.

Dominko, surrounded by men and women in suits, is speaking through the microphone. His voice cracks through the speakers. I wonder how he has been able to keep it up for so long, but I guess talking is something Dominko was always good at.

"He's not too bad," Liam says, nodding toward Dominko. I screw my nose up. I prefer the old buffoon than this pompous ass barking orders, but he seems to have the soldiers under control, and the suits don't seem to be revolting against him. I guess the important thing is that he makes sure his father doesn't get back into control and that the harvesting is stopped.

I catch my breath. The harvesting! It's day already! I turn to Liam, making eye contact with him for the first time since he kissed me. "The City," I gasp.

"Dominko sent soldiers with cease and desist orders. The harvesters have been ordered back to Headquarters to wait for Dominko and new instructions."

"New instructions?" What does that mean? They can't continue harvesting in any way!

"They will need a new direction, or there will be problems. Dominko will find alternate jobs befitting their skills."

I take a deep breath. "He seems to have everything under control."

"He's been planning this take over for as long as Ollie and Drimmy have been planning a revolt. None of them were just going to stand by and let Carlos get away with his slaughter."

I frown up at Dominko. "I never would have expected it of him."

"No, neither would I." The dryness in Liam's voice pulls a smile from me despite my bruised heart.

"I still haven't found the little people."

"Chances are, they never came anywhere near the training ground. Their mission was in the tunnels and basements. If everyone was here, they might have evaded capture."

I nod my head as hope fills me. He's right. My friends from The City had been caught, but Liam had released them while I was talking to Carlos. But the little people would have steered clear of all the soldiers.

I look back at Dominko. He would know exactly where he'd sent the little people. He's too busy bossing people around though, so I follow Liam at a jog, weaving through soldiers back toward the buildings.

We've only just rounded the corner of the first building when Liam stops, turns and tackles me to the ground.

"What are you doing?" I ask, not sure whether to laugh or pull my gun out.

He's not laughing though. He's lying on top of me, squeezing the breath from my lungs and frowning down at me. He raises his arm and wipes the back of his neck. His hand comes away bloody.

His frown deepens. "No dart."

"What is wrong with you?" I ask as he rolls off me and aims his gun at the surrounding buildings.

It's a snicker that first alerts me to Gollum's presence. A smile leaps to my face.

"They're here!" I exclaim. "Where are you? It's safe to come out."

"It's never safe with him around," Gollum replies as he leaps down from an open window. "What have I told you about running around alone with nasty men?"

"To make sure I dress appropriately."

Gollum tilts his head to the side with a furrowed brow. "No, I don't think that was it."

"No? Must have been Dominko who told me that."

"I don't know whether to be more disturbed by the thought that you could confuse me with Dominko or that you would listen to any advice he would give you."

"Hmm. They're equally concerning, I'd say."

"You threw a rock at me," Liam whines, rubbing more blood from his neck.

"Be thankful that's all I threw," Gollum growls.

I know I should stick up for Liam. There's a lot they don't know or understand about Liam's behavior back at the cave, but I decide it can wait. I'm not feeling very charitable toward him at the moment.

I skip in a circle, squealing with relief. "You're all okay!" I resist lifting Gollum or any of the other little people who've joined us into a bear hug.

"It looks like everything is under control out there," says Chartona.

I nod and screw up my nose. "Dominko seems to have stepped into his father's shoes with no trouble at all."

"Well, that's a good thing, isn't it?" Gollum asks.

I shrug and turn away, looking toward the compound exit. "I wonder if we can head back to Finn's yet?"

"We need to get out of the sun, now that we know you're all alright," replies Chartona. The little people are all wearing black scarves around their eyes, topped by large black sunglasses. I wouldn't be able to see at all, but they seem to be doing alright. They've got hands over their brows, though, to block the sun further.

I nod. "Let's go then," I reply.

"You can't come our way. Dominko gave us a map of underground tunnels that will get us to within a few blocks of Finn's. You won't fit through any of the tunnels out of the compound."

"Oh, okay," my shoulders slump. I spent so much time with the little people and then had to leave them. I've really missed them. I've only just got them back, and I don't want to let them out of my sight. "I'll see you back there then."

They nod and start running on their short legs toward another set of buildings. I watch them go until the last of them disappears inside and turn back toward the training yard. I'm brought to a sudden halt by Liam's chest. I hadn't realized he was standing so close.

I look up into his piercing eyes. Why does he have to look at me like that? It just kills me. My throat catches as he takes hold of the tops of my arms and pulls me closer. He leans down, and his lips meet mine. He begins kissing me, but I manage to get a hand up onto his chest and push him back.

"Why are you kissing me?" I ask.

His lips curve in a smile. "Out of all the reactions I thought I could get, I didn't think of that one."

I look around the empty space between buildings. "I'm not walking about in a daze about to unleash energy to hundreds of soldiers? There's no one we need to act a part for? So, what am I about to do wrong now that you need to distract me from?"

He shakes his head at me and leans down to kiss me again. Okay, so that wasn't the response I was expecting. Still, I don't mind it. Maybe, I'll protest when he's finished.

Chapter 36

"There's just so much to do; so much to undo," says Dominko as he paces in Finn's living room.

Finn nods in understanding. "I know you'll do a good job. You're not your father's son."

"Thank God for that," interjects Dominko.

"Oh, I do. Believe me, I've spent enough hours praying for you. Fortunately, despite your resistance, you have received a lot of training for the role you've assumed, and although you've shed your father's attitudes, you do have a lot of his political abilities," says Finn.

Dominko nods. "I'm just glad I had so much support in declaring my father incompetent. Now, he won't just be locked away for the rest of his life for his crimes against clones, but I can take full control of Clone Industries without any interference." Dominko smiles at me. "Your keeping him so weak he was virtually incoherent, really helped with that," he says.

"That, and the fact the other business leaders thought you'd be easy to manipulate, and too lazy and inept to run the business on your own," murmurs Liam.

Dominko turned a huge smile on him as if he'd been complimented. "The one thing Carlos did do right was to make sure he had more money and power than anyone else in the country. Now that his will has taken effect, none of them have any power over me. I just wish we could prove more of them complicit with the harvesting. I know a lot of them were blackmailed, but there were some who were fully behind it."

"We will see that the worst perpetrators are brought to justice," says Liam from beside me. His arm hangs loosely around my shoulders. I snuggle a little closer, and he tightens his hold. He's barely left my side for the last three days, which I guess is typical behavior for him, but it's different now that I can kiss him whenever I want. Well, when there's no one else around. I get too many jokes from my friends and family to want to kiss him in front of them too often.

"Between your researching and computer abilities and Finn's sources, we should be able to get enough evidence against them. At the very least, they won't be able to do anything like this again. We will have a careful watch on them, and you will have the power to stop them," Liam continues.

Dominko shakes his head. "Too much power. I can't say I like it. The thought of being anything like Carlos terrifies me. I can't just give it to someone else though. I need to fix things. But, where do I start? Finn, what would you do?"

Finn looks surprised at the question. A bubble of warmth fills me. Dominko might just be able to do this well.

"You're asking me?" says Finn.

Dominko nods and leans forward, a look of earnestness on his face and a new hope that wasn't there before. "Yes, Yes. What would you do?"

Finn considers, and after a while says, "I would appoint a board."

Dominko leans back in dismay. "A board?" he whines. "All they do is argue, "Look into things,"" he says with air quotes, "And stop me from doing anything useful."

"Well, you don't have to give them any power if you don't want to, but it would be helpful for you to, at least, have an advisory committee," Finn replies.

Dominko looks doubtful. "I don't know if I want the advice of the people who were in Carlos' ear all those years. As far as I can tell, they're almost as bad as him. I want things to be different, and the other big business leaders in Hollowcrest don't want that."

"No, you're absolutely right," Finn replies. "But, I wasn't thinking of them."

Dominko's brow furrows. "Then who?"

"A wide representation would be good, I think. It seems to me it would be good to have some clones on the board."

Dominko shakes his head. "Clones aren't engineered with those kinds of capabilities, and even if I were to start some now, it would be twenty years before they'd be old enough to begin helping. And even if that were a good option, I've lost my taste for engineering. I'm wondering if I should put a stop to it, at least within Clone Industries. Ha! Imagine that, Clone Industries, not doing cloning."

"That is an admirable thought, Dominko," says Finn. Dominko beams at the praise. "But I wasn't thinking of regular clones. There are many clones who refused to follow the descriptions written for them," replies Finn.

"Unviables?" Dominko asks.

Finn's mouth sours at the name, but Dominko doesn't notice. "Yes! Yes! You're right! Sample, you could be an advisor. You're smart and come up with great ideas and solutions!"

"Umm, I think Ollie would be better," I say, but Dominko isn't listening.

"We could have lots of unviables. And you, Finn. You have to be my advisor. And, I know another man in The City. I should be able to get him out of there now. I need to get everyone out of there."

Ollie sputters. "There would be chaos," he looks to Finn for support, but Finn is smiling at Dominko and doesn't notice him.

"I'll have an advisory committee to help me work out the logistics." Dominko waves Ollie's objection away.

"We could start by making living conditions there better and providing more food," I say.

"And give people the freedom to come and go as they please," says Drimmy.

"We'll pull down the Wall!" exclaims Dominko.

"All in good time," says Finn. "As you say Dominko, you will have an advisory committee to help you work out the logistics."

Dominko is nodding enthusiastically when Bianka walks into the room. His eyes light up at the sight of her, but he turns away immediately saying, "Yes, Yes. There is a lot to work out."

"I think you should allow clones to get an education beyond what they were engineered for. I would love to study medicine. The human body is so fascinating. Of course, I learned all about the nerves and pleasure centers of the body, but I've always wanted to learn more. It's incredible what the body is capable of."

Dominko's eyes are back on her, and this time he doesn't try to conceal his avid interest. He leaps from the lounge he's perched on the edge of, and reaches her side. "I've been studying the brain most recently. Do you know there are almost 100,000 miles of blood vessels in the brain?"

Bianka gazes up at him with keen interest.

"I still think it would be a mistake to let the unviables into Hollowcrest on any major scale," says Ollie.

"Come now Ollie, how many times have we had this conversation? Surely, you don't still think clones are morally inferior to everyone else?" asks Finn.

"No, I know you're right. I've seen what the people can do, but there could be riots or anything," Ollie replies.

"You've spent the last few weeks organizing a riot!" says Drimmy.

"Yes, yes, but that was different," Ollie paces back and forward in agitation. "That had to be done. We had to protect The City from Carlos, but that was a riot that would be contained by The City Wall. What you're suggesting could get innocent people killed. And clones! There is so much fear and prejudice against unviables."

"No, you are right," says Finn. "But, so is Dominko." He smiles at Dominko, but he and Bianka are so engrossed in their talk about body organs, he's oblivious to anyone else in the room. "Dominko's aims are the end goal, and we will work toward them with all our strength, but we will do it in a way that brings about justice for all clones, as quickly as possible, without causing chaos or injury."

I smile at Finn. That's what he always does. With the strength and mercy of his God, who I think is becoming mine, he fights for justice for people while keeping them in safety until it can be achieved.

"Want to go for a walk?" Liam breathes in my ear. Tingles run the length of my body. I leap to my feet and pull him after me. I'm eager to be outside, not just because I want to talk more with him about how he's adored me ever since he first set eyes on me, but also because I can walk the streets of Hollowcrest now without fear.

The End

Afterword

This is the end of this series for now but, if you haven't already read it, check out Melina's other series <u>The Caris Chronicles</u>.

You can also follow Melina on <u>facebook</u> at mel.grace.71 to find out when new releases come out.

Acknowledgements

A huge thank you to my beta readers Steve Mathisen from Odd Sock Proofreading and Copyediting, Valerie Medhurst, and Mal Smith. You guys rock and have made this book so much better than it would have been without you. Thanks to Juan Padron, book designer, for the awesome covers. Thank you to my readers for encouraging me to keep writing when life gets busy. I love hearing your reactions to the characters in my books. As always, thank you to my wonderful family for your unwavering love, support, and encouragement. And lastly, but never least, thanks to my heavenly father who inspires me, heals me, and shows me all the beauty he has put in people.

About the author

Melina Grace lives in Australia with her husband, two kids, and a two and a half meter carpet snake that sleeps in the roof. After 40 years of excessive daydreaming and storytelling she is very grateful to now write for a wider audience than her friends and family, who often seem to think her imagination borders on the edge of certifiably insane.

Printed in Poland
by Amazon Fulfillment
Poland Sp. z o.o., Wrocław